LAST STAND MESA

LAST STAND MESA

L. L. FOREMAN

WHEELER
CHIVERS

This Large Print edition is published by Wheeler Publishing, Waterville,
Maine, USA and by BBC Audiobooks Ltd, Bath, England.
Wheeler Publishing, a part of Gale, Cengage Learning.
Copyright © 1969 by L. L. Foreman.
The moral right of the author has been asserted.

LIBRARY OF CONGRESS CATALOGING-IN-PUBLICATION DATA

Foreman, L. L. (Leonard London), 1901–
  Last stand Mesa / by L.L. Foreman.
    p. cm. — (Wheeler Publishing large print western)
  ISBN-13: 978-1-4104-2605-5 (alk. paper)
  ISBN-10: 1-4104-2605-X (alk. paper)
  1. Cattle stealing—Fiction. 2. Fugitives from justice—Fiction.
3. Large type books. I. Title.
PS3511.O427L37 2010
813'.54—dc22   2010003206

BRITISH LIBRARY CATALOGUING-IN-PUBLICATION DATA AVAILABLE

Published in 2010 in the U.S. by arrangement with Golden West
Literary Agency.
Published in 2010 in the U.K. by arrangement with Golden West
Literary Agency.

U.K. Hardcover: 978 1 408 49110 2 (Chivers Large Print)
U.K. Softcover: 978 1 408 49111 9 (Camden Large Print)

Printed in the United States of America
1 2 3 4 5 6 7 14 13 12 11 10

LAST STAND MESA

I
LOST AND GONE

It was at Penasco that Mike McLean at last faced the conclusion that his long flight was finished. He could escape no farther. Penasco was the closed door, the end of his trail. Where the Rio Bravo made its final loop southward from the old Ford Craig ruin down to Mesilla and thence to Mexico, the great bulge of country that it embraced lay as a high plain slanted toward that river of numerous men's turbulent destinies. Yellow clumps of flowering *chamiso* patched the bare, sun-glazed surface of the plain, defying heat and lack of moisture. Some browned grass and weeds, too sparse to graze, thinly furred the higher levels up toward the sharp-cliffed mountains that walled the east.

Few men traveled this barren route south, preferring to follow the loop of the river with its narrow hem of greenery — few except men who wished to avoid the notice of the river-hugging settlements and such law as might be watching the road, used by the monthly stage. Mike McLean chose the plain.

He guessed he might have made it over the stage road, the shorter route, with benefit to his horse and to himself. It was scarcely likely that the hunters would be on the lookout for him there. Not yet. Soon, though, they'd figure it out, ask questions, cut his sign again . . .

His flight had been aimed straight for Alamogordo, the new town full of Easterners and Britishers, where he might lift a fresh horse. Then on up through the mountain passes over into Texas and a straight run to Mexico. It was his logical course, and the hunters after him knew it. A matter of simply staying ahead of them. Speed. Disregard aching muscles and sore eyes. Keep on going. Speed.

What the hunters didn't know was that he had got delayed. They thundered past him in the dark, on the bleak edge of the Lava Beds, those blackly ugly out-croppings, upraised monstrosities of nature. His delay was the fault of a Mexican goat-herder.

That damnfool *cabrero!* Broke his leg clambering after a no-account *chivo* bleating its silly kid-goat despair in a tight

8

crevice. Nothing else to do, of course, but lug the fool to his cabin and fix him up. Rule of the range.

Later that night, with the certainty by then that the posses would be guarding all mountain passes to Texas, Mike McLean had decided upon an abrupt shift in his line of flight. It had to be done.

"Mil gracias!" The old goat-herder lay on his rawhide cot, food and water within his reach on the earthen floor, an unshaded lamp-wick flickering.

From gone days he recognized the look of a hard-pressed fugitive: the quietly controlled anxiety, the air of constant listening, the faraway eyes.

Fervently, he said, "*Vaya con Dios, hijo mío!* — God go with you, my son!"

To the thanks, Mike replied, "*De nada* — it is nothing."

As for the blessing, he thought grimly: *Not God. It's the Devil who goes with me.*

He rolled a few cigarettes for the injured man. "I go now. To those who may come asking of me — you will tell nothing?"

"God strike me dead if I breathe one whisper!"

"Adiós."

He cut westward from there, abandoning the deadly course to Texas. He crossed the

San Andres by night and dropped down onto the plain in bright morning sunshine. The plain showed a vast emptiness. No distant feathers of dust pursued him. There were no dots of riders to left or right, racing to cut him off, spurred by the price of his capture dead or alive.

He breathed deeply and quit damning the delay at the Lava Beds. His luck was strained, but maybe it was still good for another notch. Crossing the San Andres in the dark had been hell, with shelving rock and loose shale threatening steep falls any minute of the nerve-racking night. They wouldn't figure he'd have tried that suicidally desperate course, much less made it on a tiring mount. He stroked a hard palm on the neck of his dun horse. The dun flicked its ears a fraction.

"You're okay," he told it aloud. "You're about played out, like me, but your heart's big. I get courage from you, the guts to keep going."

The animal didn't raise its drooping head. "Somewhere, somehow," the man said, "I've got to get a fresh horse. I'll have to turn you loose. Then it's *vaya con Dios,* eh?"

He talked for the sake of hearing a human voice in the solitude, for he was not a loner by nature. Loneliness had been imposed upon him by circumstances, particularly of late, since the circumstances outlawed him.

"I don't know this piece of country much," he said, partly to himself, partly to the horse. The horse didn't respond, plodding onward down the slant of plain. "It looks nice. Private, anyhow. We'll take it easy for a spell."

It felt good to drift along in the sun, at ease for once, after the harried days and nights behind him. Mexico was his best bet, the only bet left, if he could get there. Ahead, below the Cristobals, stretched the *Jornada de la Muerte,* journey of death by thirst.

He recalled hearing that nobody in his right mind tackled the *Jornada de la Muerte* without stout wagons, spare animals, and brimming-full water casks. And prayer.

He shrugged. Prayer alone would have to do for his equipment, if he could remember how to pray.

That night he made a dry camp near Penasco, a town of which he'd heard only rumors. Next morning he rode in, pressed by the need for water and grub for himself and the horse. He timed his arrival with the sun's high rising, when stores were open and a stranger might make purchases without drawing attention.

His timing was wrong.

As soon as he entered Penasco, Mike McLean sensed a sharpness, an element of tension in the town. Vigilance set the price that he had to pay for the privilege to live. He sent his stare searching. The prospects of impending trouble weren't hard to detect, the symptoms visible.

At this hour the *viejos,* the old men of the town, should have been gravely warming their bones in the sun, in the little plaza, thinking comfortably of their first glass of wine for the day — from tiny grapes, fermented, homemade, fortified with a strong dash of tequila.

This was the heart of the land of *Poco Tiempo,* where time sauntered drowsily. Yet the slumber could be occasionally awakened for a lively spell, and many times had been; for this also was cattle country — and cattlemen never slept, as anyone knew.

The plaza of Penasco was deserted, not a soul in sight. Explosive events lurked in the unnatural hush. Somebody was coming due for a rigged jackpot.

Me? Mike McLean speculated, thinking it highly possible.

He held the dun to its walk through the dusty little plaza. There was nothing to be gained by turning back now, and he had skinned through too many close scrapes not to have developed a degree of fatalism. If Penasco meant his finish, well, then, he was finished. He was weary of running. There weren't any horses at the hitch-racks. It was then he faced the conclusion that this was the end.

He angled over to a narrow sidestreet off the plaza, sighting down it a building that resembled a livery stable. The street was scarcely more than an alley, the fronts of adobe houses facing flush onto it, so silent that the dun's hoofbeats raised echoes. On the building that he had sighted, a weathered signboard proclaimed it to be the Bluebell Bar — C. Stuart, Proprietor. Mr. Stuart was evidently a jingo Scotsman far from home. There were a good many Scots here in the Southwest, mostly in cattle and trade. Mike McLean, of North Irish stock way back before the Revolution, didn't cotton to them much.

A livery stable adjoined the saloon, and it also was owned, its sign said, by C. Stuart, who apparently tolerated its intrusive stink and buzzing horseflies in his barroom. Across the street squatted a blacksmith shed built of unplaned slab-boards that the sun had shrunk and warped into bare ribs.

Three men lounged at the gaping door of the livery stable, fronting the street. They wore guns, McLean noted instantly; wore them in skimpy cutaway holsters, butts protruding handily. But their chilly regard was fixed on one man who stood near the sagging door of the blacksmith shed on the opposite side of the street.

Not me, McLean thought, sizing up the situation. *Not this time.* It didn't concern him, this budding shoot-out among strangers. He had his own problems. With grain and water for the dun on his mind, he pushed on to pass between the armed trio and the lone man, giving them a short nod to let them know that he was entirely neutral in their affair.

The three pairs of eyes scanned him, then leveled again at the lone man outside the blacksmith shed.

The lone man, too, glanced up, his expression rueful and faintly hopeful. He was a rakish-looking old ruffian, clad in a threadbare frock coat, shabby trousers, cracked shoes. A fake diamond, glass, flashed feebly on the chest of his soiled white shirt. His silk top hat had as many creases as a concertina.

Plain as day, he was a tinhorn cardsharp, at present badly down-at-heel due to bad luck or the bottle. His puffed eyes and shapeless red wad of a nose bespoke a long and thorough devotion to booze. Mike charitably hoped that he ran true to type and packed a loaded derringer up his sleeve. It was a bad trio bracing him. The hush of the town had its source in their coldly homicidal eyes.

Perceiving Mike's intention to pass, they exchanged rapid glances. The old tinhorn heaved a sigh. He fished out a stub of cigar, and in lighting it he slid back the threadbare cuff of his left sleeve an inch or two. The lighted match trembled in his cupped hands, but the expression on his life-battered face now reflected sad resignation, an acceptance of the fact that he had to play poor cards against aces in a stacked deal.

Mike took notice, and contempt soured his opinion of the trio. Three gun-toughs pitted against a broken-down old relic, and there they waited for a further advantage to favor them. He moved abreast of them on the dun. The livery stable was his destination and damned if he'd turn back out of their way.

They eased forward, closing in, using him and the dun as a screen. The maneuver eliminated their risk to a minimum. It made a calculated business of the kill. The derelict gambler stopped chewing on his cigar stub, as if holding his breath. He straightened up, and for that moment he displayed a touch of grandeur, a caricature of shabby elegance, an almost regal defiance to defeat and death.

It was that, as much as anything, which caused Mike McLean to rein in the dun. He said to the three in a biting rasp, "Hey, haul off! Don't rig me up for your cover!"

They eyed him, paying a closer inspection to what kind of man he was. In their preoccupation with strategy they had taken his coming simply as a chance asset. Now his voice and presence suddenly became challengingly instrusive. They saw that he was large, though gaunt, and that his sunken eyes held the marble stare of a tired man who was pushing himself. Between the eyebrows a small scar like a crooked dent gave him a permanent frown. His hair was the color of wet sand.

He was unshaved, unwashed, dusty. His holstered gun and heavily shell-studded belt looked reasonably clean — the only gear about him that still bore evidence of care.

A hardcase on the long dodge; the kind that occasionally dropped into Penasco for a brief rest and a fresh horse if they could manage it. The quiet kind that departed unobtrusively, peering constantly backward as they rode on south toward the *Jornada* and Mexico. They had to be desperate to tackle that route without a good outfit. Bleached bones made landmarks, when not buried by sandstorms.

Penasco was the last oasis, the stepping-off place on the final stretch to the border. On their way, caution compelled them to avoid unnecessary trouble.

The gun-team three, on their own stamping ground, weren't under any such compulsion. One, a youth whose hot eyes flared a craving to kill, rapped, "Get a move on, pilgrim!" He took a kick at the dun's belly, in the assurance that a longrider, no matter how tough, wasn't likely to make an issue of it.

Mike McLean reacted instinctively, resenting that foul treatment of the long-suffering animal.

He spun the dun horse, thrust out a stirruped boot, and plucked his gun clear of its cut-down leather. The gun, a heavy Colt's Walker conversion, long in the barrel, speared its red roar as the dun skittered around, but not at the youth. That young killer flailed in the dust on his back, knocked there by the outthrust boot.

A big-brimmed Texas hat sailed off,

17

slapped by Mike's bullet for fair warning. Its owner grabbed for it, turning. Mike McLean's boot caught him hinderly and sent him floundering in a header against the livery stable. The big gun blared again, smashing away the drawn gun of an older man and breaking his fingers. The threesome knew then they had braced a tiger.

The old tinhorn gambler came forward in a shambling run, calling, "Stranger, here we go!" He pitched off a shot from a sleeve-gun that was about the size of a railroad conductor's pocket watch, but with a two-barreled caliber big enough to wipe clean with a finger.

The member of the trio who was abruptly minus his hat ducked low while he dug at his holster. Mike McLean clouted him with a long sweep of his gun barrel and laid him out. The tinhorn got off a second load that jackknifed the youth gasping to his knees.

The town marshal, a stout man cradling a shotgun, barged into the street. Doors were slamming open, loosing armed citizens who plainly didn't appreciate a stranger's wrecking of local talent.

Mike McLean quit the fracas, heeling the dun on down the street. The tinhorn cried after him, "Wait for me!"

"To hell with you!" Mike grunted.

Farewell to all prospects of grain, grub, and a spell of much-needed rest. It had to be the *Jornada* for him on a worn-out horse, no food or water. He damned in his mind the busted old tinhorn, as he had damned the injured Mexican *cabrero;* and damned himself for getting involved. Would he never learn to ignore the misfortunes of others, he who bore a load of misfortune of his own?

"A hell of a life, this!" he muttered, dusting south out of aroused Penasco, more sorry for the suffering dun than for his tired and hungry self. "Horse, I apologize. That was my fault. Can't lay it to bad luck. Just bad judgment." He released a deep sigh. "I guess we're lost and gone!"

II
LAND OF
GUN-PROMISE

Glancing backward, clear of the hostile town, he spied the dust-feather of a rider pattering along his trail into the desert. In no mood to ruin the dun in a race, he reined up and waited, reloading his gun, preparing for a shootout with that sticky pursuer in the silence of the barren desert. Sixty miles of the worst desert lay ahead of Mike McLean; he wasn't going to watch his back-trail for all of it.

The single rider on his trail turned out to be the old tinhorn gambler. The horse he rode, admitted the gambler cheerily, was one he had succeeded in borrowing without the consent of its unknown owner, from the livery stable. He had laced on a saddle hurriedly in the confusion and prudently decamped.

"Me wee pistol shot itself off in the doin's," he said in a fruity Irish brogue. "Pure accident, ye unnerstand, but it left the town marshal yelpin' wid a hole in his leg, poor man! Ah, the pity of it, him mebbe the father o' childer an' all!" He wiped a bleary eye. "Me name, sir, is O'Burrifergus. Timothy Sean Mario O'Burrifergus. God knows how the Mario got in there, less'n me dear mother — rest her soul — found a soft spot in her large heart for some Eyetalian or other. 'Ould Burro,' friends called me, friends I had in the past. 'Ould Burro,' the easy touch."

"Mike McLean, me."

Ould Burro doffed his disreputable silk hat with a flourish worthy of a grandee meeting royalty. "Michael McLean, Esquire, a true gintleman an' I don't doubt a scholar! Ye head for Mexico? Well, they're foine folks, out southern neighbors. Broadminded, eh?"

"Yeah."

"But ye'll not be gittin' to Mexico by this hellish route, on a weary horse an' yerself plainly worn down. Yer bones would decorate the lonely wayside, I fear, an' mine too. A most unworthy fate for the likes of yer esteemed self, Mr. McLean, though fit enough for me."

"I didn't invite you along," Mike said.

"I took the invitation for granted," replied Ould Burro airily. "Those three bully-boys had me cold, till you hotted it up."

"Guess they must've had reason."

"Well, I'd sorta taken up for a woman they were raggin' in the saloon, an' one thing led to another. Purely personal an' unprofessional. A matter of common chivalry, though she wasn't a lady by far. On top of it, I'd stayed too long in Penasco an' wore out me welcome — as you did in remarkable short time!"

"I'd say we're both in a fix, then," Mike observed. "We can't make it south, but we sure can't go back. Any ideas?"

Ould Burro replaced his hat on his head. "Mr. McLean, you pose our problem in admirably succinct words," he responded elaborately. "This is a hostile land. 'Tis in me mind to hie hence to greener pastures, friendlier surroundings — a place mebbe more suitable to our special talents, not mentioning our health!"

"Get to the point!"

"The point is, we'd do best to slant our course over an' strike for the Llano Fuentes range. In fact, it's the only course left to us."

"And what's there?"

"Cattle country, where some kind o' range feud is going on without benefit o' law. No law left there at all, I've heard. The right place for us, *no es verdad, señor?*"

"*Es verdad!* D'you know the direction?"

"That I do," said Ould Burro. "Mr. McLean, I've got a bottle in me pocket wantin' serious attention. Let's drink a toast to the future, to life's everlastin' promise. Here's the bottle."

That night they made a hungry camp and finished the bottle.

Late morning of the next day, Ould Burro reined his stolen horse to a halt. "Divilish hot," he husked. "I'm dry as hell's bones, an' not a drink in the house." He was squinting forward, his bloodshot eyes slitted against the sun's glare. "What would those fellers comin' yonder want with us? Surely it's not the law. No lawmen here on the Llano Fuentes, less'n I was sadly misinformed."

Two approaching riders hauled in and waited for Mike and Ould Burro to come up. They put their horses broadside in clear indication of barring the way. Their impassive faces and stiff manner hinted sharply of authority. Far behind them over the rolling, brown-grassed range, a group of riders trooped westward at a walk.

"Where you headed and what's your business?"

The demand came with harsh offensiveness. Mike met the stare of brittle eyes. Bleakly, from cow-country habit, he inspected their horses. Good big animals, both wearing the same brand, a Triangle T. To the query he gave a dry retort.

"We're headed more or less yonderly, and our business is minding our own. What's yours?"

They took stock of him, up and down. The one who had rapped the demand gave his verdict, with contempt. "A raggedy dodger and a busted tinhorn, coyoting for easy pickings!"

He was large, but not stout, a man of muscle and full assurance in himself. His partner wasn't frail, either, although his narrow face made him appear skinny at first glance.

"Our business is keeping the range clean," the large man went on. "It's closed to your breed. This is the deadline for you! Tail off back the way you came! Savvy that? Savvy *this?*" Gunmetal winked blue in the sunlight.

Mike McLean sat motionless in his saddle, his gaze taking in the drawn gun and the man holding it lined at him. Here was as sudden and unsought a jackpot as he had ever met.

It came to McLean then that when a man carried as much sign of trouble as he did, further trouble became hard to avoid. He was like a tramp dog, fang-scarred, that couldn't expect to stray past its own kind without a snarling battle.

The narrow-faced man, speaking for the first time, murmured, "Maybe they oughta be earmarked before turning 'em loose, so they'll always remember to respect Triangle T range." He began sliding a short and heavy carbine out of his saddle scabbard, smiling, his eyes contemplating Ould Burro's somewhat prominent ears.

"Not needful!" Ould Burro protested hurriedly. "Not a bit! Yer friend's argyment, there in his hand, settles the matter! I take off me hat in respect to the Triangle T range!" He doffed his hat ceremoniously, bowing.

The trick that followed displayed practice and dexterity. It also helped to explain the dented condition of Ould Burro's hat. The hat skimmed spinning from his hand. Its brim evidently contained a steel stiffener, for it struck solidly the would-be earmarker on the thin bridge of his nose.

The large man started a surprised laugh at his partner's expense, then changed it to a grunt. His partner was rocking back in pain, tears streaming, both hands clasping his nose. And Ould Burro, capping the trick, was plucking out his murderous little derringer pistol from his sleeve.

Mike heeled the dun lunging forward. The horse still had a jump left in it, and Mike's heels dug it forth. He crashed into the Triangle T horse, knocking wild the large man's shot. Mike had his gun stroked out, and he reached far over and took a long swipe with its barrel.

The large man jerked his head away and caught the blow on the stretched side of his neck, on the tendons, and gasped. Losing knee-grip, his startled horse rearing, he lost his seat and pitched off. He knelt crouched on the ground, bare hands supporting him and his head at a crooked angle.

Retrieving his battered headgear and brushing dirt from it, Ould Burro proclaimed rather pompously, "Let it be a lesson in manners to the Triangle T, whatever the hell outfit that is! An injury I can take at gunpoint, but I draw the line at insult an' indignity! Earmark me, would ye?"

He wagged his derringer at the narrow-faced man, whose watering eyes couldn't see it. "Be a while before ye'll do more'n sniffle wi' your sniffer! They gen'rally break when I hit 'em right. I trust yours is no exception. Mr. McLean, what disposal do we make o' these ungintlemanly specimens?" He broke off to comment admiringly, "Ye fixed that feller! Break his neck?"

"No, just bent it. We take their guns," Mike said.

"The spoils o' war," Ould Burro approved. "The good Lord knows we need 'em, if yon men are pals o' these two buckos. They've turned this way."

The group of riders in the distance, altering their westward course, were approaching. They had heard the gunshot and witnessed the brief fight. Yet they rode slowly as if uncertain of their purpose.

Ould Burro quickly but efficiently stripped weapons from the two Triangle T men, including their carbines, gunbelts and sheathknives. He would have searched their pockets for extra trifles, only Mike put his foot down.

"Mr. O'Burrifergus, we stop short at stealing pocket cash!"

"Do we, now?" For once Ould Burro showed rebelliousness. "I detect an odor of hypocrisy, Mr. McLean!"

"How so?"

An Irish streak of cutting irony emerged. "How did yer high-principled self fall to the low state ye're in, less'n ye stole an' robbed somewhere?"

"It wasn't a pocket. It was a bank."

"Merely a matter of degree. A dollar or ten thousand, it's theft." The fruity brogue slipped at times, Mike noted. There was some education behind Mr. Timothy Sean Mario O'Burrifergus. Far, far behind.

To the Triangle T pair, Mike said, "I don't know who your boss is, but —"

"You'll sure as hell find out!" The one with the crick in his neck lurched to his horse and climbed aboard.

"Tell him we're going on," Mike said. "Where we go and how we get there is none of his damned concern!"

"So you think!" The disarmed pair took off, at a wide tangent from the oncoming group.

Ould Burro, strung with a collection of lethal hardware, grumbled, "Shoulda shot 'em! What breed o' wild men does this land raise? I'd no idea. Worse'n Penasco! Here they come, the other bunch."

"Be ready if they show fight."

" 'Deed, aye. It's us two against seven."

"Seven's a lucky number."

"Lucky for them!" Ould Burro seemed morosely pessimistic, perhaps pricked by dark forebodings. Mike didn't feel particularly optimistic, himself.

III
Trigger Treaty

The group of seven horsemen steadily advanced, leaving a low stream of dust that settled slowly behind in the windless air. Greener pastures? This range was baked and browned dry, as inhospitable as its inhabitants.

At an acceptably neutral distance, within speaking space, the seven shuffled to a halt. They glanced after the Triangle T pair of retreating range-cleaners, then eyed Mike McLean and Ould Burro with puzzlement. These obviously were hard-working cowmen and none too prosperous, lean, saddle gear mended, clothes patched.

Mike, who had been once a hard-working cowman, beckoned for them to come closer, seeing that they appeared to wait for the invitation. They had reason to hold back, for Ould Burro bore more firearms than three hands could manipulate. And for his own part, Mike realized, he'd scarcely pass muster anywhere as anything less than a raw-edged roughneck. The seven cowmen's eyes said mutely that they regarded him as a dangerous lobo.

They nudged forward a few paces. Among them were saddle guns; no six-shooters hung in sight. The saddle guns, or course, were for snapping shots at coyotes and other calf-killing varmints. These men weren't warlike. It seemed odd that they weren't, considering the belligerent contrast of the Triangle T pair.

Their leader, the eldest man, gazed dislikingly at Mike McLean and Ould Burro. His face was deeply furrowed by time, toil, worry. He had the frowning look of intolerance, soured through the frustrations of drought years, low beef prices, all the pressing problems of holding an outfit together in bad times.

"You pulled a fool play on those two!" he stated positively.

"So did they, on us!" Mike said. He scanned swiftly the horse brands, a mixed lot, not a Triangle T among them. "My name's McLean. Yours?"

"Peter Hardy. These are some of my neighbors. We work the Middle Range, over to the west."

"Howdy. This is Mr. O'Burrifergus."

"Mmm." Peter Hardy sent a somber look after the two Triangle T riders. "That one you clouted on the neck, he's called Art Garnett. The other is Homer Allen. They're top men in the Regulators. Roone's Regulators," he added as if the name didn't require any explanation.

"We're strangers. Never heard of 'em. A vigilante outfit?"

"Roone's Regulators are Triangle T men," Peter Hardy said. "They'll be hot on your tails when Art Garnett reports you. Don't look to us to hide you out. We already got plenty trouble with the Triangle T. An' frankly, we don't welcome outlaws."

"Well, now!" Ould Burro shoved in, so insulted by Hardy's tone that his forebodings went forgotten. "Outlaws, says he! Me good man, appearances are deceptive, as the old biddy said after kickin' the skunk. We don't carry our importance on us like jinglin' medals, to be sure, for we're modest men, Mr. McLean an' me! Also, we've suffered rough wear, yer benighted damn country bein' what it is! But when we locate the right kind o' range we seek for the cattle outfit owned by Mr. McLean —"

"Whoa, Burro, who there!" cut in Mike.

"— of which I'm the manager, then ye'll open yer eyes!" continued the old bluffer, inspired to lofty flights of purest falsehood. "Ye'll see the biggest herd ever that tracked the land! The finest horses! Aye, an' the best crew o' fightin' cowhands that ever busted open a closed range!"

"Burro!"

"Mr. McLean, ye know I'm as unassumin' as yerself! But I'll not sit silent while ye're insulted!" He was dazzled by the glory of his own lies. "Gintlemen! Ye think yon triangular teacups are tough? Hah! For the game of it, our boys'll run the likes o' them off into the *Jornada!* The sweat o' Roone's Regulators will start grass growin' where it never grew before!"

Peter Hardy blinked, awed by the grandiose claims. "You're cattlemen, scouting for a new location? Where d'you come from? If," he appended, "you don't mind me asking."

"From Texas, an' proud of it," answered Ould Burro after rapidly inspecting the seven cowmen's gear; double-rigged saddles, short hard-twist ropes tied hard and fast. "Texas, where the best cows an' horses come from — an' the best men, too!"

"Hmm, yeah. Right. We're Texans ourselves, origin'ly, years back." Peter Hardy exchanged glances with his neighbors. This, his eyes messaged, put a different light on the situation.

One of the group spoke up, in a curiously meaningful tone of voice. "Hardy, we can make room for 'em, and welcome. The Triangle T won't have to know, long's we all pin our mouths shut. Glad to have you, Mr. McLean. I'm Ed Horner. Meet Gray Adams, my partner. We own the Five Bar X. This is Boy Pete."

"Boy?" Mike shook hands with a blond young giant whose grip was ironlike.

"Pete Hardy's son. We called him Boy Pete since he was a little button," Ed Horner explained. He looked levelly at Hardy. "I vote we go right back and hold that meeting, regardless of Triangle T. Damn the Regulators! To hell with Brokus, too! Right?" He won nods of assent. "Good! Mr. McLean, you're invited to our meeting, you and Mr. — er —"

"Timothy Sean Mario O'Burrifergus," Ould Burro supplied grandly. "Yer hospitality is most warmin', after the cold reception we got from —"

"Wait a minute!" Mike broke in. The sudden about-face aroused his suspicions. Displaced Texans were always friendly toward other exiles from the Lone Star State, but they weren't usually as fraternal as this on first acquaintance. "What meeting?"

Ed Horner drew a breath to announce, "Special meeting of the Middle Range Cattlemen's Council." When he showed up with the group, Mike had ticked him off as a dispirited kind of man, a lanky individual with downcast face and defeated eyes. Now a brightening air dissipated the gloom.

"We were holding our meeting at the Caven place," Ed Horner said. "It got broke up." Again he sent a level look at Peter Hardy, almost accusingly. "The others will still be there if we jog smart."

Mike, holding back, told him, "Go ahead. Not us. We don't belong in your Cattlemen's Council."

"That's easy done. How about it, Hardy?"

"All right," Peter Hardy said reluctantly, glancing around at his neighbors and perceiving their mood. "They're members. Just honorary, though," he hedged. "And it's got to be voted and confirmed by the Council."

"Vote hereby confirmed! Let's get back to Cavens'!"

There was nothing much else to do but ride along with them, having received the honor of membership. Mike laid a dour stare on Ould Burro. He had a dark presentiment that the old reprobate's barefaced lies had manufactured more trouble. Ould Burro returned him a cheery grin, aimed at assuring him that fate was thwarted and all was rosy for the time being.

The Caven place turned out to be a ranch house of considerable size, well built, although plainly uncared-for and needing some repairs. The vacant bunkhouse and corrals showed equal evidence of neglect.

The Cavens, Lindsay and Jana, were brother and sister, Mike learned. They lived there alone, Jana keeping house as best she could, Lindsay not doing much of anything except drink. There was no crew, not a hired hand left on the place. Their father had built up a good outfit, but the life had drained out of it since his death.

Strong father–scapegrace son, Mike thought on meeting Lindsay Caven. It wasn't uncommon. *Well, we're what we are. I'm no credit to my name, either.*

Lindsay Caven had the look of a young man who was diligently exploring dissipation, without finding in its depths any release from whatever was driving him to it. Nor very much pleasure. He must have known it was ruining him, for he had an intelligent face, sensitive beneath its ravages. Perhaps he was intentionally drinking himself to death.

His sister, Jana, younger than he, had a quiet kind of prettiness along with a serious disposition. Her air of self-control seemed tense, apt to break under pressure. Mike felt sympathy for her. Jana Caven needed the support of a steady and reliable man. What she had instead was this brother, an educated failure and drunkard.

The main room of the house held nearly a score of cowmen. They all listened attentively to what Peter Hardy and Ed Horner had to say to them. Their eyes shifted constantly to Mike McLean, the stranger who had whipped Art Garnett. The stranger who owned a big herd on the move and bossed a fighting crew that could run Roone's Regulators out of the country.

"Mr. McLean's a Texas cattleman, like us," Ed Horner stated to the gathering. "He's lookin' for open range, and I bear witness he's able to fight for it! He knocked the horns offa Garnett and Allen in damn short order! I say we invite him to locate on the Middle Range."

Jana Caven and Boy Pete Hardy, standing close together, locked hands, thinking the fond action went unnoticed. It came to Mike, observing them, that love, like hate, was naked. It couldn't hide, it shone so brightly.

Boy Peter called out, "Sure, give him range!" And then he flushed redly, a youngster who had dared to raise voice among the elders.

Peter Hardy, his father, frowned at him. "No! I'm against it!" He looked all around at the men. "I've preached in our church against bloodshed, as you all know. Violence begets more violence. We're not gunmen. Would you entice this man, this outsider and his crew, into fighting for us? Shameful! I'll never vote for it. We shed our guns years ago, by common agreement. I stand by that, no matter what comes. Let a man like this move in, and it means bad trouble!"

In the babble of voices that broke out after Peter Hardy finished speaking, Mike raised a hand for attention. "This meeting was called earlier, I understand," he said. "What reason? What broke it up? I'd like to know what's going on here now that's raising the dust."

Following a silence, it was Lindsay Caven, a half-filled glass in his hand, who answered him. "Correct, Mr. McLean. This meeting started earlier. Its purpose was to try solving the problem of how to smuggle beef cattle out to market, for ready cash. We're all about broke. No solution to the problem, as usual. During our discussion, Garnett and Allen arrived, uninvited, and that put an end to it."

"They broke up a meeting of twenty or more? Just those two?" Mike scratched his stubbled jaw. "I don't get it."

Lindsay Caven chuckled and drank. "Our behavior perplexes you, eh?" His speech was a little thick, carefully enunciated, its tone ironic. "The answer is simple. We've lived here too long, growing used to peace and security, spending our aggressiveness in safe and petty ways on those nearest to us. My dearly departed father was a choice example — he sacrificed everything — including his family — to his greed for property and power, damn him! Damn his fine ranch, his proud possessions, his assumption of lordly superiority! Let it all sink to hell after him! I thank the horse that threw him and broke his neck! It set me free!"

Here were bitter undercurrents, drunkenly exposed. A living son against his dead father. Resentments channeled into the urge to destroy what the father had built and valued, perhaps valued overmuch, at cost to his humaneness. Mike, disinterested, though a trifle embarrassed for Jana in her awkward predicament, thought it time to change the subject.

"If your earlier meeting couldn't settle anything, then what's the use of this one?" he asked. "What's your big problem, anyway? Nobody's told me yet. Just some talk about Triangle T and Roone's Regulators."

Again, Lindsay Caven spoke before anyone else. "We need to drive our beef cattle to a buying market. The problem is, we're blocked in tight."

"How?"

"By the Triangle T. It's Eastern-owned, plenty of money behind it. The ranch manager is Amery Roone, who also heads the Regulators. The owners want Triangle T to expand, which means taking the Middle Range. To do it, Roone has got to squeeze us out, starve us out, anything. So he refuses us a right-of-way through Triangle T range, west, south or north. His Regulators enforce that prohibition, of course, though God knows they trespass on our range."

"What about a route east?" Mike queried.

Lindsay shook his head. "Blocked by the Brokus gang on Alta Mesa. They'd take our herd and laugh at us! We've got a very knotty problem." Smiling, he sloshed more whiskey into his glass and swallowed it in two gulps. "You might be the sword that'll cut the knots!"

"You don't say!"

"I do say, Mr. McLean. Yes, you and your mighty crew of Texas scrappers!" Something like skeptical amusement flickered in Lindsay's swimming eyes. "You are being elected to pull our chestnuts out of the fire! In return, we're offering you range we don't own. My good neighbors are glaring at me for putting it into plain words, I see. Oh, hell . . ."

He slumped into a chair, sank his head onto his crossed arms on the table, and passed out.

Mike eyed him thoughtfully before ranging a regard over the crowd. These upright men were in bad straits, otherwise they wouldn't compromise on pride and principles. Only desperation could have brought them to consider bribing an outsider to take on their fight.

Still, it was trickery under the guise of generous welcome. At least half of them had showed willingness to connive in it, until Lindsay Caven baldly revealed the deceit.

"Let's have the whole truth," Mike said. Back of his mind arose a speculation: *Could the situation be turned to profit?* He, too, was broke and desperate, much more so than any of them, though they didn't guess it. "First, does this Caven outfit own any cows at all?"

IV
CATTLE GAMBLE

His question puzzled them. "You bet it does," replied Ed Horner. "Maybe a thousand head, some not branded because Lindsay don't bother to. He despises the outfit. Lets it go to wrack'n ruin. Sold off the horses an' paid off the hands, after the old vinegaroon's funeral. 'Scuse me, Miss Jana, but your pa *was* pretty hard on Lindsay."

"Yes," Jana said. "My father was hard on anyone who didn't come up to his expectations. Lindsay — well, Lindsay takes after our mother. Never hard. She died too soon to help him."

The conversation threatened to delve into the past, so Mike asked Ed Horner brusquely, "What's the setup on those Regulators?"

"Amery Roone proposed organizing a vigilante squad, at Triangle T expense, to guard against stock thieves. We agreed. Now it's all Triangle T, and the Regulators boss

41

the country. There's no other law here — Roone makes sure o' that. He aims to squeeze us out and take over the whole Middle Range for Triangle T. As it is, he claims nearly all the range around it."

"Range law gives you the common right to drive a herd through any open range."

"Legal rights don't count here. Triangle T range is closed tight. We've tried. The Regulators turn us back. They tell us to take the east route around Alta Mesa. That's a joke."

"I don't see it," Mike said.

Ed Horner shrugged. "You're a stranger. Guess you've never heard of Bloody-wire Brokus. He rules the roost there on Alta Mesa. It'd give him a big laugh, a herd trailing right into his territory. Be like shooing chickens into a wolf-den!"

"A tough lobo, eh?"

"None tougher. Lobo's the word for him. Fits his men, too. Alta Mesa is, well, it's the kinda place where —"

"Call it a robbers' roost and be done with it!" snapped Peter Hardy. "A vile nest of gunmen, outlaws, rustlers and worse! Tell the truth, Horner!"

"They ain't robbed us, not so far."

"It's only a matter of time!"

"Maybe, Mr. Hardy, maybe. We don't

42

know it for sure." Reluctantly, Ed Horner told Mike, "We lately suspect Brokus has got his eye on the Middle Range, too, as well as on our cows."

"You sure are boxed in! Triangle T on one side, Brokus on the other, both hungering to swallow you!"

"Yeah, that's about it."

"And that's the jackpot that you'd steer an unsuspecting pilgrim into, like me!" Mike commented. "Won't you fight for what you've got?"

"We're hanging on, but we're against bloodshed."

" 'Cept you can get some fool to shed it for you!" Mike had a few more scathing words to add, but then up spoke Ould Burro.

"Gintlemen, ye're the victims o' graspin' scoundrels!" Ould Burro bugled indignantly. "A sad pass, so it is, when honest men are beset by blackguards on all sides! Me blood boils! How much longer can ye last?"

His red-veined face was innocent of guile, or as innocent as it could ever look. Mike suspected, though, that the penniless and disreputable old adventurer was feeling out the situation for possibilities of personal gain, as he himself was doing. *We're a fine pair!* he thought.

Ed Horner stroked his nose, an unconscious and tell-tale gesture of evasiveness. "Well, I dunno. It's hard to say . . ."

"Ah, stick to the truth!" broke in Boy Pete, and this time he didn't flush and withdraw. "If we don't get a beef herd out to market soon, we're all finished! Every cowman here is in debt up to his ears, bankrupt!"

Peter Hardy shook his head at his too-outspoken son, muttering that it wasn't as bad as that. To which Boy Pete retorted, "It's worse! Our credit's used up. Can't pay our bills, can you, Dad? We mend our boots, patch our clothes. . . . I'm sick of it! Sick of hanging on. Hanging on for what?"

The assembled cowmen were silent, looking gravely at Peter Hardy, who, taken aback by his son's outburst, shook his head again without speaking.

Mike said reminiscently, "I've bossed a trail herd or two through rough country." He paused. "Did you know there's a new gold strike near Torreon? A mining camp's springing up there. Tent-shacks like usual, I s'pose. Crowds of miners hungry for beef. Good market, top price. You might consider it."

They glanced at one another moodily. "We'd have to cross the river," Ed Horner

44

pointed out. "It's running high now, no ford. Too fast to swim."

"Build a log raft. Line it across with ropes. Ferry your cows over a few at a trip. Take time, but worth it to sell beef at Torreon for ready gold."

"Can't be done!" Peter Hardy stated positively. "Even if we could put a herd over the river by raft, we'd still have to go by Alta Mesa. There's no other way. Brokus would jump us. We'd lose the herd, Mr. McLean!"

"Not if I had a crew of good men," Mike responded. "Men, I said. I don't mean gunless, gutless trash. Men!"

Ed Horner slapped his hat on his knee. "By God, that's the talk! Ol' Texas talk, pure quill, an' high time we heard it! Boy Pete, I'm with you — I'm sick o' poverty, when we own cows that's worth plenty money! McLean, count me in. I was a fighty young jigger once." He stopped, to ask cautiously, "What would you want out of it, s'pose you got a herd of ours out to market?"

"Five thousand dollars, on the barrel. Failing delivery of herd to market, then no pay. Can you guarantee my price, with the cash in sight?"

"We couldn't raise five thousand cents!"

Mike nodded. "Okay, you're broke." Ould

45

Burro's eyes were on him, inquisitively crafty. "Seeing I've got nothing much now to busy me, I'll take a gamble," Mike said. "I propose you shape up a trail herd, about three thousand head. That's about the right size for a drive to Torreon. A thousand of your beef steers will be owned by me, papers signed beforehand."

He splayed a hand to a chorus of protests. "Hear me through before you blow off! The thousand head signed over to me can be Caven cows. You say Lindsay's letting the stock run wild, anyway, so I guess he'd be willing to take my note for 'em at five dollars a head. It's not a big offer, but better than nothing. If we can get the herd to market, I'll make my profit. If we can't, I lose the gamble."

They talked it over, mostly in favor although hesitant to commit themselves. One of them asked, "Wouldn't it be better to wait till your outfit gets here?"

Ould Burro handled that awkward question. "Mr. McLean an' me would have to trek far back an' guide 'em down. It'd take many days. A trail outfit the size of our NS travels very slow, on account o' grass an' water an' all," he explained glibly. "By then, some enterprisin' cowmen will have beaten us to Torreon an' glutted the market. Even

46

miners can only eat just so much beef, y'know. It's been suggested that what ye want is somebody to pull yer hot chestnuts out o' the fire. A fallacious wish, gintlemen! Whilst ye wait, yer chestnuts burn!"

Another man inquired skeptically, "How many cows can you sell in a mining camp? Not three thousand!"

"No," Mike agreed, "but Torreon's the first bet. Sell all we can there, and outfit ourselves for the trail to the northern markets. You'd come home loaded with cash."

The thought of it lured them. They held further consultation, nodding their heads in general agreement.

The vote went over the unyielding opposition of Peter Hardy, who declared, "It's a mad and dangerous scheme! It means fighting — as I'm sure you must foresee, McLean! You and your man there are hardcases, but we're not. Us older men set a peaceful example long ago. Our young men hardly know how to wear a gun belt, with the holster tied down like yours — let alone how to use a gun, like you can, no doubt!" he accused.

"It's time they learned," Mike countered. "Peace has got to be earned, like freedom. When you're not willing to earn it, and there's no legal protection for you to turn to, then you're shoved around and stepped on. And you deserve it!"

"Hear, hear!" Ould Burro applauded.

Peter Hardy addressed the meeting. "Do you follow this McLean outsider? You'll regret it! I know his reckless kind from way back. A Middle Range roundup will bring on war!"

"Since when did cowmen give up the right to hold a roundup of their own cattle on their own range?"

"It's not a matter of right, McLean! We're trying to keep the lid on, praying that one day our enemies will destroy each other in their ungodly greed!"

"Your prayers, sir, might be answered in due course," commented Ould Burro. "Wolves will fight each other over a cornered rabbit. Aye, mebbe to the death. Meantime the misfortuned rabbit lies fanged to flitters between 'em. The rabbit may gain a moral satisfaction, but much good it does him!"

"Right!" Ed Horner seconded. "Who wants to be a rabbit?"

"A dead rabbit, at that!" a cowman put in, Ould Burro's crafty analogy rankling.

It was revolt. The peace-inspired leadership of Peter Hardy lay discredited. Faith in his preaching and high-minded example suddenly collapsed. It must have been wearing thin. Others joined Ed Horner in rebellion, particularly the younger men, shouting assent while nodding at Mike McLean.

The nods implied that Mike was informally elected leader, which was more than he had bargained for. There was no vote, only the unspoken assumption that he would take charge.

Boy Pete called to him, "How about we begin the roundup tomorrow, Mr. McLean? I've got a little bunch of my own that I'll throw in for a start!"

Defeated, bitter hurt in his eyes, Peter Hardy looked at Mike. "If any harm comes to my son — if you drag him and the others into a losing fight — I think I'll kill you! Bear that in mind! I haven't always been a peaceful man."

He stumped out of the Caven house, shaking off the restraining hands of friends who sought to talk the thing over with him. At the door he snapped, either from anger or a flash of insight, "That feller might be a big cattleman but I got my doubts! To me he's a gunslinger on the make! I warn you all!"

"Now, Hardy, that's no way to —"

"Him and that old Irisher! Fly-by-nights! Wouldn't s'prise me if they're wanted!"

Cold mice-feet trod Mike's spine. One of

the friends, watching Peter Hardy march off to his horse, said uncomfortably, "Kindly overlook it, Mr. McLean. He's natch-ally sore, 'count we overruled him."

"Let's end the meeting," Ed Horner said, "an' go home. Miss Jana, you want help with Lindsay?"

"No, I can manage, thanks," the girl answered. "He'll be all right presently."

Pride, Mike thought. She wouldn't allow her brother to be lugged limply to bed like the sodden drunkard that he was. Not even by Boy Pete. She would get Lindsay to his bed by herself, and sit lonely the rest of the day. Tragedy was often quiet.

During the ride from the Caven place, the men hardly spoke. Mike guessed they were thinking of Peter Hardy. They had broken a settled pattern and taken a long step, a drastic step, and an aftermath of sober reflection subdued them. Well, they would have to grow used to taking positive action.

Middle Range had a little one-street town that for some forgotten reason was named Fifty — possibly because it was fifty miles from anywhere. Only one room could be rented in it, behind a log-built saloon titled unsurprisingly the Log Cabin Bar. It smelled musty, but was moderately clean. Ould Burro said it was mighty convenient, and after a constructive visit to the bar he joined Mike in their room.

"A poor brand o' whiskey they serve, befittin' the men who inhabit these parts," he remarked, plumping himself down on a rawhide chair. He slapped his hands on his knees. "Ye could've made a better deal, Michael. They'd have given their own notes for Caven's cattle, an' mebbe scraped up a bit o' cash to boot, they're that anxious for yer valuable services. Cash is what we're after! Ye let 'em off easy. Why?"

Mike, boots off, rubbed his feet. "I owned a ranch once. Small spread, but mine. Got rooked out of it. I hate the Roone breed."

"Sentiment's an unprofitable emotion, me friend! Lettin' suckers off easy offends me esthetic senses. I like yer gamble not one damn bit! There's no fondness in me for Mr. Peter Hardy. An upright citizen, aye. So upright, they've deposed him from the throne. But they've listened to him for a long time. They'll listen again, should ye stumble just once!"

"Quit dealing me misery!"

"They'll turn on ye in a wink! An' ye're takin' on to teach 'em how to fight? How to use guns? Lord save us!"

Mike scowled. "I think you're prejudiced."

"Prejudice," observed Ould Burro, "is

gen'rally an offspring of ignorance. Therefore ye're wrong." He drew from his coat pocket a full pint of whiskey, newly acquired on credit at the bar. "I'm not an ignorant man, Michael. As they saying goes, I know whereof I speak! Drink?"

V
KING OF ALTA MESA

Grass sprouted on Middle Range, the sun blazed down, and cowmen were up and about. Organization of the roundup was completed. Mike McLean was elected *carporal* without dissenting votes, and he chose Ed Horner and Boy Pete as his *segundos*.

Here in the deep Southwest everyone used the old-time Spanish terms. An "Anglo" cowman might be at a loss trying to converse with a Mexican *vaquero*, but he called a noseband a *bozal*, a feeding bag a *morral*, and a horsehair rope was a *mecate*, its slipknot a *honda*.

Chuck wagons had been repaired and put in order, horses gathered, some shod, and wranglers delegated to handle the remuda. Roundup crews rode to work on the beef-herd hunt. The range was large, brushy in spots, not a fence-line on it. The cattle, after too long running free, snuffily disputed any influence toward discipline. Some were as wild as deer.

There were five chuck wagons feeding forty-odd riders early breakfast and late dinner, a hasty snack in between for those able to make it. Due to the heat, cattle had congregated at the shaded outwaters, spring ponds and water holes. The drive had to spread miles out to bring them in. At the *parada* ground the work went on in clouds of dust; cutting, trail-branding, shaping up a trail herd for market.

It had to be good, the herd, to sell straight without benefit of feeder middlemen. Torreon would pay high for good beef. The owners and hired hands, all of a kind, were working together against time now. Except in dry humor, the title of *Mister* never came up, and *boss* was out of use. This was a cow camp.

The increasing herd contained all colors, black, brown, red, yellow. The sweating roundup hands sawed off horns, laid on the hot irons, did their messier work, and ran the pick into the gather. Sixteen hours a day of hard work. Sit tight the catty cutter and spin the loop nimble, drag the bawling critter to the fires and go for another. Cussing didn't help, but it seemed to.

Boy Pete proved to have a natural talent in gun practice. He could shoot fast and accurately, never bothered by nerves. He was Mike's best pupil, but he had the fault of digging his big hand downward at his holster instead of smoothly stroking the gun out upward. A fatal fault, if he ever matched draws with an expert. With all Mike's teaching, he couldn't overcome it, simple forthrightness being his nature.

Surprisingly, to Mike at least, Lindsay Caven joined the roundup and put in a share of work. Sober, he was a quiet young man, a capable rider and roper although exhaustion lined his face at day's end. He worked as if driving himself to prove to his own judgment that he could hold up his end with anybody.

More surprisingly, he outclassed the rest in sessions of gun practice. He cocked while smoothly drawing, fired promptly as the barrel came level, and rarely missed hitting the can. Respect for him, which had fallen low, rose somewhat among the Middle Range cowmen.

But he hadn't stopped his drinking, and when drunk he was sardonically merry, a jeering onlooker at life. He and Ould Burro got together every night with a jug, winding up hilarious, an irresponsible pair of nuisances keeping everybody in camp awake. Mike couldn't tell which one was the worse influence on the other. He would have ordered Lindsay out of camp, except that he had a regard for Jana Caven's feelings. He only hoped the hard work might eventually straighten out her wastrel brother. Or wear him out.

"Any coffee, Burro?" Mike called, riding over from the busy *parada* to the chuck wagons.

The beef herd was shaping up. In the cutting and branding, dust billowed, cows bawled, dirt-caked men cursed, and any horse was apt to spring a bonehead notion at a critical moment. It was a tough time for all. Tempers were taut. Lindsay Caven hadn't turned out for this day's work.

"There's the damn coffeepot," Ould Burro answered Mike sourly. "Want I should pour for yer lordship?"

He heartily despised the cook job that Mike had talked him into taking on. The job entailed entirely too much labor for his taste, and scant dignity. He was sore at Mike, disgusted with the whole business, and was hitting the jug — property of Lindsay Caven, who had brought a supply of whiskey to the roundup camp.

Lindsay sat on the ground, leaning against a wheel of the chuck wagon, drinking. Mike scowled.

The scowl registered in Ould Burro's somewhat fuddled consciousness. "If ye've got a complaint, air it!"

Mike heaved his sweaty body out of the saddle. "This blasted outfit!" He filled a tin cup with boiled coffee, bitter-black enough to mummify a corpse. "Oh, they know the work, sure. They know it all! Every order from me, they want to argue it. I wish this was a regular crew of hired hands. I'd fire a few. You, for one! A booze-bum who can't cook worth —"

"Say no more!" interrupted Ould Burro. He hurled an iron ladle at the cook fire, hitting the Dutch oven. The ladle clanged off, and Mike's ground-reined horse skipped, snorting.

"I hereby resign me lowly position!" he trumpeted, swaying to his feet. "Fully do I concur wi' Mr. Caven's opinion o' cows an' all the damnfool cowmen connected therewith!" He swung around to focus a bleary gaze on Lindsay Caven. "Lindsay, me friend, is there a shot left in that canister? I desire to celebrate me sunder from the bedamned bovine business!"

Lindsay waved the jug. "*Por si, viejo!* Come and get it. 'For let us laugh and never think, and live in the wild anarchy of drink!' I've misquoted that line, I believe, but let it go. It was what the revered Ben Jonson or somebody meant, writing with ponderous pen —"

Whatever it was that somebody meant, it went with the drifting dust, for just then Ed Horner loped over with some others from the *parada,* calling urgently, "Hey, McLean! Trouble! There's a gang comin'!" Seconds later, Ed Horner exclaimed, "Oh, Lord, it's Brokus! We're in for it!"

Mike drank his coffee. The fears and alarms of these Middle Range cowmen no longer pricked him. They cried wolf too often. Good men, exasperatingly cantankerous, but tame, they saw spooks in shadows, potential peril everywhere. Peter Hardy had taught them wrongly, made them almost timid.

Only when he grew aware of a heavy silence did Mike set down his tin cup and glance around. Ould Burro, he saw, was sidling behind the chuck wagon — a seriously significant move. Ed Horner and those with him wore the scared look of cats threatened by a pack of dogs.

Nine horsemen, newly arrived, sat gazing at the camp. The racket of the *parada* had deadened the sound of their coming. They were heavily armed, all nine, and well mounted. None of their horses bore the

Triangle T brand. Mike took in that much before giving regard to a bearded man who met his eyes with a mockingly humorous stare.

He was huge, the bearded man, bigger than Boy Pete, that young giant. He had a royal tilt to his long-haired head, supreme arrogance in the thrust of his jaw, and plainly possessed massive strength. His wide green eyes contained absolute assurance of power, like the eyes of a barbaric monarch, a conquering emperor at the head of his army. His voice roared at Mike.

"What the hell are you up to here?"

Instantly bristling, Mike rapped, "What the hell does it look like? Who the blue blazes are you?"

The bearded man shoved back his hat. "Boys," he said to his men, "this feller don't know me! He's a stranger in a strange land. Don't gun him down yet. I'm curious about him. What's your name, feller?"

"Mike McLean."

"A goddam Scotch-Irisher! I knew it! You're the sizzler who put the crick in Garnett's neck, eh? I'm Brokus. Bloodywire Brokus. I've wrecked more barbwire fence than a man could ride in a year o' paydays! Mike McLean, you're wastin' your time on this roundup. It won't pay off."

"Want to bet?"

"Don't try bluffin' me! I judge you've already bet your shirt an' saddle. You can't win! I'm sorry to say it, for I like your style. You remind me of when I started out with only a rope an' a runnin' iron."

"Why d'you figure I can't win?"

"Because your backers here won't back you all the way! You've got to depend on 'em, but they'll let you down in the pinch. You're bettin' on schoolma'ams to beat Triangle T!"

Ed Horner and the others stayed mute. A pair of Middle Range riders, bringing a roped two-year-old onto the *parada,* hauled in short. The men at the branding fires didn't move to take the steer.

"We'll make this roundup," Mike said, with more conviction than he felt. "And we'll get a herd out."

Brokus wagged his massive head indulgently. "Ah, to be young again! You do me good, McLean. It's a pity you're on the wrong side, caught in a hopeless cause. When you lose out an' these blue-bellies turn on you, come to me, hear? I'll have a place for you."

"Where? Alta Mesa?"

Brokus boomed a laugh. His men, chill-eyed, listened and looked on, unsmiling.

60

"Where else? Give us a hail as you come, an' wait for welcome. We only let in those we invite, an' that's rare. A rare honor," he added, heavy irony in his tone.

Mike, feeling that he was being mocked at, said, "I'll do without that honor. No reason I know of for it."

"No reason?" inquired a rider alongside Brokus, a slim youngster wearing a loose-fitting jacket, smooth face shaded and partly concealed by a wide-brimmed sombrero.

Mike let the query go unanswered, rather than give a trigger-itchy stripling an excuse to pull a gun on him.

The slim youngster raised a hand to the big sombrero, a slow deliberateness in the movement. Mike remembered Ould Borro's hat trick. But the sombrero came off and was slapped to knock the dust from it, then was used as a fan. The sun shone on the uncovered head of a girl, filling Mike with confusion and a sense of shocked outrage.

She had dark hair, thick and glossy. Released from under the sombrero, it cascaded in soft waves which she brushed back with a deft flick of the hand, a gesture wholly feminine. The same gesture allowed the loose-fitting jacket to gape open, revealing the firm rounds of breasts beneath her shirt, a slender waist and womanly thighs. Her

61

smooth skin had a warm, rich hue, almost dusky.

Mike automatically lifted off his own stained and fire-spotted hat. He stood bareheaded, his hair sweat-plastered and tangled and badly in need of barbering. Nobody else present paid the girl that courtesy, and Brokus' stare at Mike grew curiously blank and still.

"No reason?" she asked again.

Mike held her level gaze, scanning deeply into her dark jade-green eyes. He guessed she could be called a beauty. His mind at the moment wasn't in a state to reach a cool conclusion about her. What he did know for sure was that her presence had an extraordinarily rousing impact on him. His senses leaped.

"I take that back," he answered her. Still holding her gaze, he let his eyes frankly signal the masculine dare. "Right now I know a good reason for visiting Alta Mesa. Best reason in the world, if you live there!"

The girl crimsoned, eyes widening, lips parted in an intake of breath at his forthright meaning. Brokus exploded a laugh, whirling his horse around, and abruptly the nine rode off. His voice came bellowing back over the drumming hoofbeats.

"Watch your step, McLean!"

■ ■ ■ ■

"So that's Brokus!" he said to the Middle Range cowmen about him. "Friends, I suspect you've still been holding out on me. What kind of outfit does he run, exactly? What's his stake in your range?"

"We told you," Ed Horner answered uncomfortably.

"You told me some of it. Why do you all act rabbit when he shows up?"

The rest of the *parada* crew had come up as soon as the Brokus squad departed. Among them, Boy Pete called, "Because the honest truth is we're scared! Alta Mesa's an outlaw hangout, a refuge for wanted killers and the like. Those you just saw are a sample. Brokus takes 'em in, being an outlaw himself. No knowing how many's on his crew, but it's plenty big. For years he's raided into Texas for cattle, whole herds, an' beat off the posses. He could chew us up anytime!"

"Except only for Triangle T?"

"*Only?* Triangle T's a mighty big outfit!"

Peter Hardy who had finally and reluctantly consented to work with the roundup, put in, "Like we told you, McLean, our range is a no man's land between Alta Mesa and Triangle T. Both want it. Either one moves in, it means fighting the other. Roone wants it for Triangle T, bad. Brokus wants room to settle down like a respectable rancher. He does everything in a big way, but Triangle T's too much even for him to buck. Meantime, there ain't a chance of getting a herd out past either of 'em! Any of our cows reach market, it won't be us driving 'em! It'll be Brokus' killers or Roone's Triangle T gunhands!"

"Then what are we holding this roundup for?" Mike demanded. "Why put up a trail herd if you're so sure it'll fail?"

"Ask the others, not me," responded Peter Hardy. "I've disfavored this from the first. I only came in on it to keep peace with my son and see he don't get in trouble. Ask Ed Horner your question — he's doing the thinking for 'em!"

It put Ed Horner on the spot. "Well, it's like this, McLean," he said, contorting his leathery face in what was meant for a candid smile. "We been hopin' your outfit'd show up by the time we got our herd ready for travel. Or some o' your tough crew, anyhow, to lend a hand. They must know roughly where you are. You musta left signs for 'em to follow."

Mike stared speechlessly at Ould Burro,

who, taking a swig from Lindsay Caven's bottle, hooted, "Chestnuts!"

It was no use flying off the handle. The glib-tongued old reprobate had created a mirage of false hope for the besieged Middle Range cowmen, but with good intention, according to his view. Nor could the cowmen be blamed much for depending on that hope, without openly admitting it. Mike swallowed his anger. He had deceived them, too, aided by Ould Burro's grandiose lies.

"I guess Brokus was about right," he said, but didn't enlarge on it. "Who was the girl?"

"That's his daughter."

"Daughter? Name?"

"Flame," Ed Horner replied. "Outlandish name, but it fits. The Cheyenne Flame, we call her." He curled one side of his upper lip. "Her mother was part Cheyenne, they say, an' part French. Maybe some Mexican too, I wouldn't wonder."

Mike frowned at the display of bigoted intolerance. It became more difficult to hold his temper in check.

"A French Canadian saved my hide once," he mentioned, gazing off. "I made friends among the Cheyennes. I've ridden with Mexicans. Shared grub and smokes with 'em." He brought his gaze back to Ed Horner. "Miss Brokus strikes me as being quite some young lady."

"The Cheyenne Flame ain't what we call a lady. How could she be a lady, livin' among outlaws? Wears men's pants an' rides straddle! Looks you bold in the eye! Maybe that's what catches the men. Certain kinds o' men."

"Like me, for instance?" Mike took it up. He regarded Ed Horner thoughtfully, deciding on where to hit him if he spoke one more word out of line.

"I didn't say that!" came the quick denial. "What's come over you, McLean? Are you trying to push a fight on me?"

They were all looking strangely at Mike. "I don't like loose talk about a lady," he said, and waited.

Ed Horner nodded. "Okay." He swallowed and let a moment go by. "What's the chance your outfit turns up soon?"

"Don't bet on it!" Mike advised.

Lindsay Caven, who hadn't moved from the wagon wheel, uttered a sardonic laugh. Mike glanced swiftly at him and caught a mocking glint in his eyes. From some corner of alcoholic perception, a flash of the truth had come to Lindsay. Or else Ould Burro had let out a few careless words, enough for Lindsay to know that there wasn't any big Texas outfit coming, now or ever.

Mike was conscious of a cooling attitude toward him on the part of the cowmen, after his brush with Ed Horner. He, an outsider, had made one of them back down, and it didn't set well with them. Ed Horner's tight expression indicated choked resentment. If Lindsay Caven spilled his knowledge that the outsider was a busted fly-by-night on the make, the lid would blow off.

"Problems!" Mike muttered under his breath.

A speck of discretion urged him to pick a good horse and head forthwith for Mexico while he still had the chance. Several factors held him back from following the urge, self-respect one of them; it was all he had left. He owed the cowmen some loyalty, regardless of their faults. As long as they went on trusting him, he couldn't run out on them, quitting flat the job that he had started, and retain much of an opinion of himself.

Besides, he badly needed a stake.

He consciously omitted the girl, Flame Brokus, from his reasons for staying with the gamble. But she was on the list. . . .

"Did you say somethin'?" Ed Horner swung around, half belligerently, his confidence bolstered by a delayed recognition that he had the support of the Middle

Range group.

Mike shook his head. "No, I didn't," he replied very civilly, aiming at giving the man the satisfaction of scoring a small victory with which to salve his injured pride.

It succeeded. Ed Horner turned away, glancing around at the group. Striding to the coffeepot, he hitched up his gunbelt as if he had worn it all his life, not realizing he had copied that gesture from Mike McLean.

VI
Come to the Dance

Jana Caven drove out to the camp in a buckboard early that evening, to take her brother home. She had done it before. From past experience she was able to predict when Lindsay would be too far gone to ride a horse. Mike and Boy Pete loaded him into the buckboard.

Opening one eye, Lindsay cocked it up at Mike's face bent over him, and chuckled. "You big son'f a gun!" he mumbled, drunkenly affectionate. "Got 'em all hoodwinked, eh? Mike McLean, owner o' the mighty NS outfit — the might None Such! Your note's a joke! Bit o' paper. I'll frame it for a laugh."

Mike chilled inside. He had given his signed note in good faith, five thousand dollars for the Caven steers, on the understanding that he would pay it off after the herd was sold. He had no intention of welshing on the debt if he could possibly carry the deal through.

He avoided meeting the questioning eyes of Jana and Boy Pete, until Jana whispered dismayedly, "What did he mean by that?" Lindsay's chuckle merged into a snore. "Was he trying to say we won't be able to sell the cattle after all?"

"Seemed like it," Boy Pete muttered.

"But we must! We've *got* to have the money!"

Mike couldn't stand it. He said roughly, "We'll get the herd out! We'll sell! You'll get the money!" Rash promise, binding him tighter than ever.

He turned his back while the young pair kissed good night, both comforted by his promise, each reassuring the other murmuringly that all was going to turn out well. It gave him a pang to hear them, as well as a feeling of emptiness.

Jana drove off home with her brother curled asleep on the floorboards. Boy Pete came up beside Mike, and they stood for a minute, not speaking, watching bright patches of golden mimosa fade as the sun sank.

Then Boy Pete said very gravely, "I'm not about to ask you any pers'nal questions, Mr. McLean. I just pray you're straight, 'cause I like you. But if you let Jana down, look out!"

All Mike could find to say was, "I'll do

70

everything I can to get the herd through. My oath on it. Keep your shirt on."

Boy Pete nodded. He was terribly in earnest. "I'll keep my mouth shut, too. I mean about what Lindsay said to you. About your outfit, and the note you gave him for his cows. They're Jana's cows, too, half. I'd sure hate to believe what he said. It won't go any farther, unless —"

"Okay, Pete."

"Lindsay was awful drunk anyway, wasn't he?"

"Yeah, awful drunk. I hope somebody's fixed supper."

"Me too. I'm hungry."

The shaping up of the beef herd neared completion toward the end of that week, despite slowdowns. Mike knew that the Middle Range cowmen had stretched out the work purposely, wasting time in the hope of seeing his mighty NS crew come boiling along to help with the drive. The None Such. He called a general meeting.

"I've talked hard to myself," he told the crowd, "and I believe there's a way to get the herd out. Roone's Triangle T riders will be watching for us to start the drive. So will the Brokus mob. First sight of our trail dust, they'll be onto us. The only question then is which one of 'em jumps us, where and when. That right?"

The crowd, unresponsive, waited. His blunt statement of the facts depressed them, as he intended it should. They had to face up to the situation, cast off their gullible hope of outside aid, and realize it was swim or sink. He had to prepare them for his plan.

Lindsay Caven, sober the whole day for once, was watching him and listening closely. A genuine interest replaced his usual air of cynical detachment.

"Late at night, though," Mike said, "nobody's likely to spot the dust of a trail herd miles off in the roughs." He saw incredulity spread over the cowmen's faces. "Yeah, I know. A load of grief, starting a new trail herd off in the dark. The critters'll be spooky, hard as hell to handle. We'll lose some. But with luck we can get through and beyond Triangle T range by morning, if we push."

Peter Hardy found his voice. "McLean, you're crazy! It's the craziest idea I ever heard!"

"Tell me why."

"It can't be done! In the first place, d'you think the Triangle T goes to bed with the birds? The Regulators? Roone? An' the Brokus mob partic'ly! They're watching us day an' night! They know the herd's ready!"

"I'd be surprised if they didn't."

A dozen voices joined Peter Hardy's. "Then how — ?"

Mike held up a hand. "Kindly hear me out," he requested with more politeness than he had used for days. "I propose we announce our roundup's finished and we're all set to begin the drive Monday."

It stunned them. Lindsay Caven smiled, his eyes sharp with curiosity. Ed Horner exclaimed, "What? Give 'em notice?"

"Sure! And we give a dance somewhere to celebrate before we hit the trail. It's an old Texas custom, in case you've forgot. A big Saturday night *baile.* Everybody invited. Welcome all, more the better!"

"Now we know he's crazy!" muttered Peter Hardy.

Lindsay, however, said, "Go on, Mr. McLean! Then what?"

"Thank you, Mr. Caven," Mike acknowledged. "When the *baile* gets going good, then we slip out, two, three at a time. We hurry back here and start the drive right away. It'll be the one night nobody expects us to work. Did anybody ever quit a good *baile,* to go fool with cows? I ask you!"

The younger men grinned. So did some of the older ones, eyes pensively stirred by the faraway memories of laughing girls, swishing skirts, lively music. It was long since the folks of Middle Range had held a dance, a *baile* with all the trimmings — too long.

"Friends, neighbors, and others!" Lindsay Caven spoke up. "I hereby announce a dance at my place Saturday night! Spread the tidings hither and yon. Come one, come all, and bring the ladies! Burro, prince of guzzlers, what became of my last bottle?"

"Lindsay, baron o' boozers, we killed it!"

"You did? Oh, well . . ."

Mike didn't intend going to the dance himself. He had too much to think about, he told the cowmen on Saturday. Let them cut the capers, just so long as they remembered to get back soon after midnight. Especially the younger men; they were to watch the time and not get high, bearing in mind the real, secret reason for the *baile.* He would be waiting for them.

His dedication to stern duty impressed them. They regarded him with renewed respect as a man who was able to control his human inclinations and temptations.

The truth was, he owned no other clothes than he had on, worn and ripped to rags during the roundup. The knees of his pants, unprotected by chaps, were split open and tied with string, and the remnants of his shirt barely covered him. He couldn't admit to the cowmen that he hadn't the cash to buy a new outfit in Fifty.

So he stayed in camp, while the men departed on their various ways homeward to get spruced up and escort their womenfolk to the party. They rode off in high spirits, most of them, looking forward to it. They couldn't help welcoming the break in the barren monotony of their lives, even though for them the party couldn't last longer than midnight, which was usually when a *baile* hit its top stride.

The midnight deadline caused Lindsay Caven to toss off a witty reference to Cinderella's twelve o'clock curfew. It raised a laugh. Boy Pete raised another, saying Cinderella didn't have to hurry off and start driving a herd of cows in the dark.

Four elderly cowhands, bribed and cajoled into taking night guard duty, circled the herd, crooning tunelessly. Every so often one of them would come in for a go at the coffee pot by the fire, then give Mike a grunt and drift on back.

At the chuck wagon Ould Burro was settled down with a pint flask that Lindsay Caven had charitably slipped to him. Lindsay possessed a drunkard's knack for hiding bottles in unlikely places, and seemed never to be totally out of whiskey.

In spite of his stern resolution, Mike found his thoughts straying constantly to the *baile.* Sitting alone at the cook fire, chain-smoking, he kept shifting his position like an insomniac in bed, unable to find comfort for long. He got up, stretched, sat down again, and poured himself another mug of scalding black coffee that he didn't particularly want. It tasted bitter. He grumpily emptied the tin mug onto the ground. In imagination he could see and hear the Caven shindig.

Lights and music and laughter. The dancing. Girls' bright eyes and flushed faces, skirts swirling, feet twinkling, a glimpse of legs here and there . . .

"Damn!" he muttered, getting up and stretching again.

It had been a long time.

"Michael," Ould Burro growled amiably from where he sat leaning against a wagon wheel, "ye're twitchy as a matin' bird! Ye're that restless ye disturb the quiet flow o' me philosophical musin's. All work an' no play is yer trouble. It'll ruin the best o' men."

"What would you know about that, old-timer?"

"I was a young buck once meself, full o' ginger an' energy. Aye, an' ambition, as I recall. I was also gifted wi' the good sense never to miss a dance if I could help it, no matter me condition. Go to it, man! This bloody camp needs ye no more'n a graveyard needs a brass band."

"Well, I don't know —" Mike demurred, more than half persuaded.

"I've diagnosed yer ailment correctly, Michael. On that I'll stake me professional reputation. I've prescribed the remedy, which ye owe to yerself to take in copious measures, limited only by the extent of suchever female willingness as may —"

"Don't go into details!" Mike caught up his saddle and gear. "Guess maybe I ought to see how it's going along, at that. I won't be gone long. I'll try to pick up another pint for you from Lindsay."

"A generous thought! Payment for me professional diagnostical consultation!" Ould Burro shook his flask. "This'n should last me an hour or two yet, so take time an' have all the fun ye can. Ye've earned it, Lord knows, an' be damned to the blue-nosed likes o' Peter Hardy!"

VII
BULLET BAILE

Mike heard the music from afar off. When he reached the Caven place the *baile* appeared to be going along fine, in pretty full blast considering the hour.

All he would do, he'd promised himself, was take a look. Nothing more, notwithstanding Ould Burro's prescription and broad-minded suggestions. No involvement. A window would do. Just a look from outside, a minute to listen, then depart. Even that wasn't strictly necessary, except for his own pleasure — it was so damned lonely out at the cow camp.

Horses and rigs crowded the yard. Some older cowmen had a fire going and were grouped at it, passing a jug around, drinking sparingly, talking of cattle and the weather and the state of the range. Peter Hardy was one of them, severe and unsmiling whenever someone cracked a mildly ribald joke. He didn't notice Mike's arrival.

A few elderly matrons stayed together in the rigs, their gossip a confidential murmuring.

Inside the house, hanging lamps shed a mellow light. Men dressed in their Sunday best stood along the walls, eyes roving. The women, far outnumbered as usual, had their pick of dancing partners. Unmarried girls were princesses this night, the plainest of them made to feel beautiful by eager young men.

At one end of the main room, opposite the musicians and a leather-lunged caller, sat the inevitable row of watchful ladies, self-appointed chaperones who guarded the proprieties. The Death Watch. They nodded approval to plain and prim girls who didn't show an ankle. They exchanged whispered censure on the pretty and popular girls, those who happened to lack the advantage of being related to them. It was a real *baile,* nothing missing, a good time enjoyed by all.

How he chanced to get inside, Mike wasn't sure. Somehow, after tying his horse and posting himself at a window, he got caught in a mixed crowd of new arrivals pushing into the front door. His powers of resistance having weakened, he went on in with them, feeling that it wasn't polite to struggle against the happy tide.

Girls' flowered dresses and men's colored shirts presented a constantly changing pattern on the dance floor. Mike kept close to the wall and behind the line of extra men, acutely conscious of his disreputable appearance.

The musicians were a fiddler and a guitar player, both Mexican, dandied up in the finery of ruffled shirts, tight pants, short velvet jackets elaborately brocaded with silver. They managed to insert traces of Mexican rhythm into the square dance.

Mike soon figured he had to leave the party. It was too much for him. It made him tingle, wishing he were scrubbed and shaved, spruced up like the other men, able to prance over to a pretty girl and request the honor and pleasure. He'd had his look. Time to go.

The press at the front entrance was a jam. He edged on along the wall toward a door at the rear that would let him go through the house and out the back, unnoticed, he hoped. Back to the cows for him.

He overheard a man he passed behind exclaim to another, "Look who's coming in! *Them!* Dammit, they know they ain't welcome here!"

Occupied in easing unobtrusively along

the wall, Mike suddenly realized that the rear door had opened for a file of entering newcomers. It took only a glance for him to know what they were, by their manner alone if nothing else. They marched in, coldly inspecting the crowd, like power-bloated law officers. There were eight of them: Roone's Regulators.

Shoving people aside, they ranged in line, and then they resembled a squad of executioners. Garnett was one of the eight unwelcome guests. He still had a swollen knot on his neck that tilted his head. His eyes, brilliantly malevolent, fastened on Mike.

"Hiya, there, stranger!" he called, and silence spread.

The Regulators didn't move, yet they gave Mike the impression of stiffening to attention, as if on signal. Lack of visible weapons didn't mean anything. Their coats bulged. Mike had left off his gun, respecting the common rule against going armed to a social gathering that involved women.

"Hi." Mike returned Garnett's greeting neutrally. He moved on, careful not to hurry. A show of haste would prompt them to act. He hoped to stall off trouble by easing out of the house. The eight had come primed for trouble.

Near the rear door somebody said softly,

"Not that way, McLean! There are four more waiting out back!" It was Lindsay Caven. Mike felt the butt of a gun nudge him.

He took the gun and thrust it under his shirt. The Regulators were watching him from behind. "What d'you reckon they're here for?"

"I'm afraid they've come looking for you — and with a secondary purpose of breaking up this party. The women aren't greatly alarmed yet. Some of these people don't realize there's anything much wrong. But if anything happens it'll be sheer hell in here!" Lindsay paused as Ed Horner joined them.

Ed Horner whispered bitterly to Mike, "You said you'd stay in camp! They wouldn'ta come if you'd stayed away! Garnett's got it in for you, an' he's their leader. They're ripe to bust loose, on account o' you!"

"In this mixed crowd, in a private home?"

"Anywhere! What do they care? All these women, God help us! Get out, will you? Those gun-hounds won't leave long's you're here!"

"I'll try and bait 'em out after me," Mike said.

"Dammit, Horner!" Lindsay protested. "You're putting it up to him to walk out to his death! There are four more outside! Twelve to one!"

"It beats havin' a shoot-out in here. A panic."

"It does," Mike agreed with Ed Horner, and he asked Lindsay, "You got any better way?"

Lindsay looked at him. He slowly shook his head. "Good luck, friend," he said in a voice that meant goodbye.

"Yeah. Keep the party going."

The rear door wasn't the way out, with four Regulators covering the back of the house. Mike began circling around the room toward the front entrance. A quick glance told him that Garnett's squad followed in his course, except for one man who slipped out through the rear door. They came pushing on, creating a stir along the crowded walls where guests waited for the next dance.

A whisper reached him from Boy Pete, standing with Jana Caven. "Watch out, Mr. McLean! One's gone to —"

"I know."

"They'll run round to the front."

"I know."

"Can I do anything? Can I help?"

He had two friends, anyway. Lindsay Caven and Boy Pete, among all the Middle

Range cowmen, were willing to stick their necks out for him, forgiving his mistake in coming to the *baile,* a mistake he didn't forgive in himself.

"No, Pete, you can't help," he said, to Jana Caven's grateful relief. "Don't try."

The Regulators, now seven, were catching up, stalking him. He moved on faster, dropping the pretense of casualness, intent on drawing them outside to do their shooting in the yard, not within the houseful of women and unarmed men. He touched the gun that Lindsay had given him, under his tattered shirt. A Colt Frontier .44 single-action, from the feel of it.

Abreast of the two musicians and the caller, who was fortifying his throat on a drink, Mike stopped, his exit cut off by a disturbance at the front door. The men there, a packed clot of onlookers, were making way for new guests coming in late. They were turning to stare, strange expressions on their faces, at the incomers.

A cowman near Mike exclaimed, "No, it can't be!" And in the next breath, "It's her, by God! The Cheyenne Flame!"

What the invasion of grim Regulators had failed to do so far, the Cheyenne Flame accomplished by merely stepping through the door. She caught and held instant attention.

Her presence stopped the party.

In the crushing hush, only she retained an appearance of cool poise. The inhospitably staring eyes must have conveyed to her — as cruelly as a slap in the face, Mike thought — the miserable truth of how these people judged her. She was an outcast, unwelcome among them, shunned.

Yet she stood erect, head high, betraying no sign of knowing that her arrival, to their minds, was an act of blatant impertinence. On the contrary, she looked as completely bulwarked with pride as a young queen, and as royally self-possessed.

She wore no hoydenish range garb this night. For the occasion she was all girl, clad in feminine finery; a girl who knew the art of adornment, grace, charm, for men to admire and women to hate.

Her gown was the color of turquoise, the clean and vivid sky-blue turquoise beloved by the Navajo and Taoseño. The tight bodice fitted closely the swell of her breasts and slenderness of waist, and the upper folds of the flowing skirt hinted of rounded hips. She wore her hair piled high, crowned with a Spanish comb encrusted with turquoise stones the exact shade of her gown.

That much Mike took in fast. At their one brief meeting he had been strongly attracted, but now his senses leaped. Hers was the beauty of polished ivory, of crystal tourmaline, of lustrous opal. He had once seen a collection of precious gems and fine carvings. The experience had widened and deepened his appreciation of genuine beauty, making him for some time afterward chary of painted lulus.

There was something else about her that his senses detected. Beneath that cool poise of surface composure, she was fighting to hold onto her nerve, as hard as any gunfighter in a long-odds jackpot. She had foreseen rejection, yet had come here to the *baile,* perhaps hoping that in the unguarded hours of gaiety the frigid intolerance might relent a little.

It wasn't blatant impertinence and brazen effrontery that brought her here, Mike believed. She lived in a hangout of lawless men, the daughter of a veteran lobo chief. Alta Mesa, being what it was, was womanless except for herself — and possibly a transient female once in a while, tramp lulus.

She couldn't help having a girl's natural dreams and yearnings. It must, Mike guessed, be terribly lonely for her up there on Alta Mesa, that feared and shunned roost, nobody of her own sex to talk to and confide in. He knew about loneliness.

His thoughts exploded in a rush of anger at the staring men and women under the hanging lamps. Couldn't they see she wanted their friendship? *Offer her a decent greeting! Damn you, she's paying you an honor! Who the hell d'you think you are?*

He met her gaze across the heads of people between them, he being taller than average. For a second it seemed to him that her eyes shed off their cool mask, and warmed as if she was glad to see him, if only as a friend in hostile surroundings. He warmed in swift return, showing it, but she lowered her eyes.

He took note then of the four men following her into the big room. Alta Mesa men, openly armed. Her gunslung escort of bodyguards.

One of the four stepped close to her and cupped his hand under her arm. A man of good manners, though not of good morals or he wouldn't belong in Alta Mesa. He was tall and lean, strikingly handsome. His garb, rakishly elegant — red string-tie, black pants and jacket — was enhanced by a gold concho that held together the dangling chinstrings of his Mexican sombrero.

He had been one of the riders with Brokus, visiting the Middle Range roundup camp. Mike later heard him spoken of by name as Colorado Jack, one-time leader of a road agent gang, now *caporal* for Brokus. His gang had got wiped out robbing an Army paymaster, and the Federals wanted him.

Smiling, Colorado Jack led the Cheyenne Flame forward onto the dance floor. He had a superb sureness of himself, no question of that, his every movement springily graceful, a bit overly graceful, left hand on hip and elbow cocked out. It went wasted, however. The fiddler and the guitar player, smelling trouble, were discreetly packing to leave the *gringo* party. Dancers, vacating the floor, whispered uneasily to one another.

Colorado Jack looked up from the face of the girl beside him, a swift scowl replacing his smile. By reputation he was a dangerous man for a crowd such as this to snub. As the floor cleared he then saw the Regulators standing halted along the wall to his left, watching him. For an instant his whole body visibly snapped taut.

They were strung out, taking advantage of unwilling shelter behind some of the guests. They had shifted their attention from Mike, concentrating it on Colorado Jack and the trio of Alta Mesa men who had followed him in. The enmity between the Triangle T and Alta Mesa wasn't an affair of grudges. Control of all the Llano Fuentes range was the prize, no truce at any time. The Middle Range cowmen didn't count. The winner would run them out. Rumor had it that both Roone and Brokus offered cash bounties for slain members of each other's crew.

In the next instant Colorado Jack smiled, seemingly relaxed. Removing his hand from the girl's arm, he motioned behind him to the Alta Mesa trio, who had taken up positions in the doorway. They sent darting stares over the room, spotted the reason for his signal, and stepped apart. They had come openly armed, like Colorado Jack.

The women grew aware of the tension, its cause, and the impending clash. The sharp-eyed chaperones of the Death Watch caught on first. One of them smothered a scream, hands over her wrinkled mouth.

The scream sounded gibbery and foolish, but it stamped a stark reality onto disaster in the making. Men's faces grayed. Gunfire in this crowded room meant panic. Someone among the gunmen was sure to blaze away indiscriminately, keyed-up and wolf-wild. A gunfight here would wreak as much tragic damage as an explosion of dynamite.

Unhurriedly, Colorado Jack turned with the girl and sauntered to the front door.

Reaching it, he swung around, making a dashing figure, his glance twinkling darkly at Garnett and the Regulators, his fingertips tapping a tattoo on his brace of holsters.

Mike inwardly cursed the man's foolhardy pride. The Alta Mesa *caporal* wasn't big enough to back sensibly out of a ruinous showdown. With a crowd and a lovely girl for audience, he had to stage a grand exit, though it risked the lives of frightened women. The Regulators couldn't be expected to tolerate his swaggering arrogance.

In the touch-and-go moment, Mike spoke to the Mexican guitarist. "Strike up a dance, *amigo!* Quick, play something! Play" — for some reason he could think of no other tune than — " 'Festivo del Diablo.' "

It was a hell of a choice: "The Devil's Holiday."

Astonished, the musician automatically cradled his huge guitar and hit the strings. The sonorous ring of the opening chord brought all eyes to him. The fiddler hesitated, shrugged resignedly, fitted the heel of his violin under his chin, and joined in.

A hell of tune, by turns subtle and savage, plaintive and then bold. Probably nobody here knew how to dance to its changing beat — the slow glides and sudden whirls of a Spanish *gitano* waltz composed long before

Emperor Maximilian attempted to introduce a refining French taste into the culture of an ancient race.

Mike struck across the floor. The clack of his boot heels beat an unconscious metronome, spacing the music's tempo, double time. He was between the two opposing forces of gunmen when they fastened their eyes on him questioningly, not knowing what he was up to.

The eyes of the Cheyenne Flame also fastened on him. Unlike those of other women in the room, hers weren't frantic, he saw. The gaze she gave him was understanding. Stopping before her, he inclined his head, gravely formal, forgetting the incongruity of his deplorable rags. He ignored Colorado Jack's amazed glare at him.

"May I have the pleasure of this dance?"

VIII
THREE'S A CROWD

He took her hand, she offering it readily, and led her forward from the Alta Mesa escort. Colorado Jack drew a harsh breath of outraged objection. Mike glanced back at him and murmured a perfunctory, *"Con permiso,"* which broadly could have meant he had her permission to take the liberty, not necessarily *his* permission.

He stepped out with her onto the emptied floor.

Music and lights, a girl in his arms, skirts swirling, face flushed. He had spent time in Old Mexico, and evidently so had she. They swung easily together into the rhythm, the two musicians taking interest and playing up to them. Her bare arm was smooth to his roughened hand. Her waist yielded to his guiding pressure. He sensed a warm and vibrant life running deep in her. Fire ambushed behind her jade-green eyes.

He was a man who had his share of faults,

vices, Adam instincts, and impulses good and bad. Her closeness and her scent swept peril from his mind. He could have forgotten the gunmen, if some clumsy blockhead, bulling out, hadn't crashed over a chair.

The music and their dance had gained the effect he'd sought, creating a diversion, breaking the frozen tenseness. Fear was still rampant, but panic lessened. The guests, women, first, were swarming out the front door. Colorado Jack and his trio stood apart to let the crowd cram past. The Regulators held to their stations along the wall.

The two Mexican musicians played on, watching the door for a chance to streak out. They knew the pattern of the game. There was going to be a shooting when the crowd cleared out. They weren't shy of a shooting, but this was none of their affair, and their instruments were — *ai, por Dios!* — fragile and costly.

Still dancing, whirling the girl lightly around, Mike guided her toward the wall that the ladies of the Death Watch had vacated. "We'll have to take that side window," he murmured to her. "Sorry. Got no choice."

He wished they could continue the dance to its stirring *gitano* climax. She tilted back her head to look up into his face. "Don't be sorry. I'm not." Her voice was low-toned, warm.

In her shining eyes he plumbed a spirit that made light of hazards. She possessed a gay courage, perhaps recklessness.

"I've never broken out of anywhere through a window before," she confided. "You don't know what a quiet and guarded life mine is, actually."

"Your life's still guarded," Mike said. "By me." His arm pressed her unresisting waist. "I don't guarantee the quiet part of it."

An impatient trigger suddenly exploded a shell that promptly changed the Caven home into a madhouse. The last tail-end of guests, men who had herded the women ahead, burst on out through the door in a brief scramble to safety. The two musicians streaked after them, running a gauntlet of gunfire, clutching their precious instruments.

The four Alta Mesa men crouched shooting, not flinching from the odds against them. Through a rising screen of smoke Colorado Jack even flashed a white-toothed grin over his pair of thudding guns.

The Regulators, splitting up and spreading out, firing on the move, displayed a similar chill efficiency, inhuman. One of them stumbled, raising a hand halfway to his head, and fell. The others didn't pay him the slightest heed.

Garnett came trotting along the wall, bent low, on his toes. Seeing him coming, glimpsing the expression on his face, Mike dug out the gun that Lindsay Caven had slipped to him. Garnett, halting at the unexpected sight of it, dived to the floor while he hurriedly fired. The knot in his neck had evidently impaired his nerve, possibly his muscle control as well, for he missed the mark and Mike heard Flame utter a small cry.

Mike slammed a shot that cured Garnett of the knot and anything else that ailed him. A crash of window glass brought him twisting around, mindful of the other Regulators outdoors, and worried by Flame's cry, but it was she who was smashing the window, with a chair. The ladies of the Death Watch had closed the window tightly against the night draft on their backs, and the quickest remedy was to smash it. Flame didn't appear to have suffered damage from Garnett's bullet, except that her high Spanish comb was gone.

Mike helped her through the wrecked window and got out after her, on the side of the house. The gunfire in the main room thundered on without letup. The front yard was a wild pandemonium of frantic women, shouting men, and rearing horses scared senseless by the prolonged outburst. Mike pulled Flame farther away from the light of the window.

"Did you drive here in a rig?" he asked her.

She shook her head, while fingering her hair for bits of the bullet-shattered comb. "There aren't any wheeled rigs up on Alta Mesa. My horse is tied to the fence out front, with Colorado Jack's and the others' — unless it's bolted off by now." She extracted a stray comb-tooth from her hair. "If that bullet had been much lower —" Her voice quickened in warning. "Watch out! Rear corner!"

Mike flicked a look and made out two figures coming around from the dark rear of the house. The lamps of the main room were getting shot out in the fight, but the window still shed enough light for the shimmering turquoise gown to reflect faintly, although Flame stood motionless in shadow. Yet the two oncoming Regulators, intent on using the window to fire through, nearly reached it before the gown distracted them.

They paused, peering. The foremost one advanced slowly, obviously unsure of whatever else the shadows might hold, but lured onward to investigate the gowned figure. "Come here!" he ordered, then grunted startledly, a different kind of figure looming up, leaping at him.

The upswing of his gun wasn't finished when Mike struck him down. The second man backed a step, saying a hurried, "No, no!" to Mike's pointblank gun muzzle. He turned and fled.

"They're not all brave," Flame said. She stooped and took the downed man's gun.

"Not all crazy," Mike amended. "Come on!"

The front yard was emptying in a boil of noisy confusion. Men on foot dodged the wheels of women-laden rigs careening out fast. Horsemen fought plunging mounts, and tethered horses were trying their hardest to snap ropes and bridle reins. They were all infected with panic, humans and animals alike, as if the gunmen battling in the house might charge forth any minute to commit mass slaughter.

Peter Hardy, leading a group of Middle Range cowmen, was striving to impose some semblence of order and sanity onto the chaotic exodus. He spied Mike and Flame, and planted himself in their path. Rage at first held him speechless. When the words came they were wildly immoderate for him.

"You trouble-making tramp, McLean!" he shouted. "You hoodlum! Gunslinger! This is your doing!"

"I didn't come here tonight for trouble of any kind," Mike disclaimed. "How was I to know there'd be a shootout? Those fellers didn't know it themselves till they —"

"You brought it on!" Peter Hardy insisted, deaf to any rational argument. "Your kind always brings on trouble!"

"I did all I could to stall it off and give the folks time to —"

"Liar! I saw what you did!" Rage, fastening onto Mike as the scapegoat, couldn't be reasoned with. "You got hold of a gun somewhere. Call that stalling off trouble? You danced shameless with this Brokus hussy showing her legs like a —"

Mike sliced his gun up, changed his mind immediately, and struck with his left fist. Peter Hardy rolled back and several hands caught him. He breathed heavily, shaking his head. "I don't like to hit an older man," Mike said soberly, "but he asked for it. He used the wrong words."

"So you defend her good name!" Ed Horner sneered angrily. "You're taking up for her — or taking up *with* her, eh?"

"Want my answer to that?" Mike asked

him, and Horner clamped his mouth shut."

Flame turned swiftly away. Gathering up the skirt of her gown, without waiting for aid she mounted a restlessly stamping sorrel that instantly bowed its neck and uncorked its temper as if it had all the wide world to buck in. Flame stayed in the saddle, her piled hair tumbling loose with the sorrel's jolting jumps, skirt and petticoats flying.

Mike's cowhorse, discomposed by the excitement, also had to throw a bone-shaking fit before allowing its rider any saddle comfort. The Caven front yard was in a worse turmoil than ever by the time Mike and Flame got their horses under control and loping away from there. Behind them, the last of the house lamps blinked out.

A waning quarter-moon etched the folds of the land in pale silver and black, making cobwebs of the *chamiso* bushes. The stands of tall cactus were ghosts; the pacing hooves of the two horses rustled quietly in the dry grass.

Ahead, Alta Mesa towered higher and bulkier as the distance shrank. Its plunging cliffs, darkly gashed by age-old arroyos and criss-crossed with bared outcrops of rim-rock, looked utterly inaccessible. A nature-made fortress.

Mike scanned the forbidding great *barrancas* of Alta Mesa while he and Flame walked their horses side by side. Those sheer walls seemed impossible for anything but a goat to climb. But he knew how the eye could be deceived in this country of rolling plains and abrupt mountains, blue haze, false shadows, mirages. Especially at night.

And the girl was sure of the route. She rode with her face turned upward to the night sky as if meditating about something that had nothing to do with cliffs.

Breaking a long silence, she said, "I shouldn't have gone to the dance, I know. They think I went for devilment, of course. To spoil it for them. The Cheyenne Flame — the Brokus hussy. . . . But they're all wrong. I went to the dance because I — well, because —" She gave her head a slight shake and didn't go on.

"I know," Mike said, and she flashed him a glance. "Same reason I went. Lonesome. It's me they're mostly blaming for what happened, till they get cooled off."

"I hope the Caven house didn't burn down. Those broken oil lamps —"

"Yeah. If it did, Colorado Jack might be on a hot route to a hotter place. That part of it wouldn't upset my sleep, to be frank. You worried about him?"

She smiled. "Not a bit."

"Glad to hear it," Mike said. He doubted if many of the partisans in that madly blazing gunfight had survived uninjured.

Presently, both of them hearing a rapid patter of hoofbeats in the brooding stillness, Flame said, "That's most probably Colorado Jack. We'll soon know, the rate he's coming after us. He'll give his yell when he sights us, and that'll be before we sight him. He can see in the dark like a cat. A wildcat," she added. "He never fails to turn up, usually without a scratch on him. It's a miracle how he does it. I think he must have sold his soul to the Devil."

They reined in, listening to the increasing pounding of a furiously ridden horse. The rider was giving the animal no mercy, spurring it hard, quirt flaying. A wild yell rang out, like the crescendo of a coyote's nighthunt howl. Moments later the onrushing horse and rider came hurtling at Mike and Flame. Mike touched the gun in his belt.

Colorado Jack swerved hard around them, plowing up clods of dirt, and hauled to a jolting halt. He laughed, misreading Mike's wince as a sign of nerves. It was for the cruelly abused horse that Mike winced. Such showy riding, ruining the animal's tender mouth, was senselessly brutal after the punishment of spurs and quirt.

Colorado Jack's eyes shone and glinted like the polished gold concho dangling under his chin. His brittle laugh, too, gave evidence of a rabid mood. He was keyed-up with the aftermath of the night's violence, drunk on bloodshed.

"Hello, *querida mía,*" he drawled to Flame. He cuffed his sombrero up and leaned forward on his saddle horn. "We sure busted that party! Enjoy yourself?"

"How are the others?" she asked him.

He shrugged, spreading one hand in a wide gesture. "They're not complainin'. Nor some of those Triangle T Regulators, who got regulated to hell. I was last to leave the party — as per my usual style an' habit, not to mention my reputation for walkin' away with a whole skin."

"Walking? You rode as if hell was catching up behind you!"

"No *querida mía,* I was catching up with heaven." He jerked his chin dismissingly at Mike. "You can go now! I got delayed at the party, but here I am to perform my proper social duty. G'night!"

Mike said carefully, "Social duty weighs with me, too. Giving the case full consideration from all sides to the middle, I don't see how I can properly get out of escorting

Miss Brokus the rest of the way home."

The top gunman of Alta Mesa eased upright in his saddle. "It's a point," he allowed softly, "but don't push it! I don't like you, to begin with."

"The feeling's mutual."

"It wouldn't take much for me to —"

"You're forgetting one thing," Flame interrupted. "You forget that I have something to say about this." In her right hand she held the gun that she had taken from the downed Regulator.

Colorado Jack switched his gaze to her, and dropped it to the gun. It was pointed at his gold concho. "Would you shoot me, *querida?* Aw, no!"

"I would!" she responded. "Don't call me *querida* again. Not ever. I don't like that, coming from you." Her tone contained cool authority. "If Dad heard, he'd run you off."

"Now, look! I took you the *baile* —"

"You and three others. On Dad's orders. Because he wouldn't allow me to go alone — least of all alone with you, anywhere! And I'm not riding back alone with you, either, so don't argue! I ride with Mike."

Colorado Jack stared fixedly at her. The pale moonlight showed his face quivering spasmodically, maniacal. Mike tensed, ready to draw and shoot faster than he'd ever done in his life, sure that the man's fury must burst berserk. A monstrous vanity had been pricked.

The hammer of Flame's gun clicked to full cock. "Don't you dare!"

Colorado Jack gusted a harsh breath. He reined his sweating and foam-flecked horse savagely over, spurred it, and tore off. As he rocketed past Mike he didn't even glance at him. His eyes glared straight ahead like those of a rabid dog. With that puncture in his vanity, and the hangover of violence, there was no knowing where he'd go and what he'd do in some insane act to unleash rage and repair his egotism.

Mike let his hand fall from the butt of his holstered gun, and looked at Flame. "Is he always that crazy?"

"When he can't have his own way, yes. Tonight was the worst."

"Had his own way too often, maybe," Mike commented.

"I guess so, until he came to Alta Mesa. He stays on because he's high on the wanted lists in too many places."

"I doubt it's his only reason. He's *muy macho,* if you know the meaning. For you."

Color tinged her cheeks. "I know the meaning. He's also *muy malo.* But Dad can handle him and keep him in line. Dad's had his way a good while longer than Colorado Jack."

Her words indicated a rather casual acceptance of a way of life in which raw might and lawlessness ruled and danger was a common element. Yet it was apparent that she found that kind of life less than satisfactory. She had the wish to live in a more normal fashion. Mike surmised that she had done so at some time, for her speech and manners were anything but coarse or hoydenish. She was an astonishing mixture.

They rode on side by side, saying little more, and their silence itself became a strengthening bond. They glanced aside at each other, exchanging smiles without any spoken reason. There was no reason to talk. It passed from Mike's mind that he was a hunted man trying desperately to raise a stake. He clean forgot that.

IX
FIGHTERS OF FIFTY

The closer they approached Alta Mesa, the more silent Flame became. She ceased to smile, growing subdued and withdrawn, the huge bulk seeming to crush her spirits and force her to a sense of grim reality. Her mood disturbed Mike. Soon they would part, and he didn't want this night to end on a low note of sadness. He couldn't yet perceive a feasible ascent up the cliffs, and wondered why Flame didn't turn off from the direct approach.

Reading his thoughts, she said, "The trail up to the top is on the south side slope, about a mile from here. It's guarded. To-night I'll take my private path. I discovered it two years ago, after a freak cloudburst. The heavy rain had cut it. I kept it a secret to myself."

"Why?" Mike asked her.

"Because I thought that the day may come when I'd need it. An escape route. Dad can't last forever. He rules over a wild bunch. He takes risks. Should anything happen to him . . ." She lifted her slim shoulders in a shrug that was weirdly like that of a fatalistic gunman.

Mike nodded. A chill touched his spine. "Then Colorado Jack would take over. Or somebody like him."

"Yes. They're badmen, some worse than others. That's why I'm avoiding the regular trail tonight. The men on guard there might get reckless with me. I'll not take the risk."

"Your father's more than reckless, risking you in a pack of wolves! He ought to think of your future!"

"Nobody knows the future," she said, souding tiredly defensive. "Dad believes he's — well, indestructible."

"Then he's as crazy as Colorado Jack!" Mike snapped.

She shrugged again. "I suppose we're all what life makes of us. Dad has lived a wild life in many places. He has many bad faults. But he's not crazy."

Reaching the foot of the mesa, she pointed. "There's the first arroyo. They cut into one another, and my path sort of zigzags up them to the top. Most of the way I'll have to lead my horse, it's so steep. We part here, Mike."

He looked up the cliff, trying to trace her secret path. "Supposing I came up some time to call on you?"

"No. Nobody comes uninvited to Alta Mesa. You'd be shot the minute you showed yourself." She gazed gravely into his face. "But thank you. And for the dance, everything."

"Wait!" He nudged his horse after her. "Soon's I get back from the drive, I want to see you."

"The drive? She shook her head. "That will be too late, maybe weeks off. By then, I'm afraid, I'll be married."

"Married!"

"To Mr. Roone of Triangle T."

He laughed shortly in relief, taking her statement as a joke. "You rattled me for a minute! Good night, Flame."

"Good night, Mike," she called back somberly.

Watching until she passed from sight up beyond a rising bend of the arroyo, he wondered why she had spoken so strangely. The thought was fantastic — marriage between her and Brokus' mortal enemy, Roone, boss of Triangle T and the Regulators. A peculiar joke for her to make, and she had not been in a joking mood.

He was strongly tempted to start up the

arroyo after her, but reckoned he'd better not. It might jeopardize her secret path to discovery by the alert men of Alta Mesa. Besides, the time was due for the night drive of the Middle Range herd to begin.

She was gone, and the schedule ruled that he wouldn't see her again for weeks, maybe never if the drive went wrong. Mike turned his horse, feeling more desolate than he'd ever felt in his life, haunted by vague forebodings in which the cattle drive took on the aspect of an impossible task, the Middle Range struggle for survival a lost cause, his gamble a failure.

Black pessimism was as rare to him as an admission of defeat. He was still a young man, as years counted, years crammed with experience, not all good nor all bad. He regarded struggle as simply a part of life.

His parents' education hadn't fitted them to cope with tough country, and he'd buried both of them when just a boy. After that, having nothing left to tie him to the hard-scrabble San Saba homestead, he left to make his own way.

Perhaps as a recompense, nature gave him the body of a strong and healthy male, vigorous, able to do a man's job at fifteen and ride back with his head not lolling. Nature couldn't erase the bad days from his young memory, though, or ease harsh days ahead. Nor could it save him from developing a tough frame of mind, a tough philosophy so close to cynicism that the degree of difference couldn't be measured.

Mike McLean was a tough and cynical man, and he knew it. Not heartless — he didn't have to be that. Heartlessness was for the weak and spitefully vicious, on the whole. But he had never heard gentle words addressed to him, as he could recall, since boyhood. Never seen the soft shine of a woman's eyes turned trustingly to him. There had been women, but not that kind. He guessed he had missed out on much that some men took for granted.

He drew away from Alta Mesa while attempting to overcome his depression by meditating on Flame, daughter of an outlaw chief, outlaws her only acquaintances. Was she genuine? *Dammit, I'm way out of law myself!* he remembered. *Who am I to judge anybody?*

The reminder jerked his wandering mind back to solid realities. Cash-value realities. Cattle. The profit on a thousand head of beef steers was his if he could get them to a buying market. Five, ten dollars a head, maybe more. He stood to win anywhere from five thousand dollars on up. Enough of a stake for a fresh start in some far-off place where . . .

A sudden rumbling sounded like thunder over the range. But thunder didn't make that sound. It was made by running, bawling cattle.

He rode into a roundup camp that guarded nothing but the empty *parada* ground and an expanse of empty, dust-hung range. The herd was gone and so was the remuda, not a cow or a horse left, nothing to show for the long days of hard work.

Staring about him, Mike cursed in a dreary monotone, numbed by the catastrophe. Even in his cursing, he let the stark fact hit home that he was at fault.

He shouldn't have left camp to go to the *baile.* Shouldn't have stayed away so long. God knew what he could have done to stop the stampede, probably only got himself trampled to death, but the herd was his responsibility and that was that.

From underneath the chuck wagon Ould Burro called hoarsely to him, "Well, there y'are, Michael, cussin' a blue streak, the whole outfit gone to hell! I knew yer gamble wouldn't pay, the odds so ridiculous tall!"

"What happened?" Mike snapped at the old reprobate. "What set off the stampede?"

111

"Does it matter now? Ye better take a deep seat in the saddle for a far destination! Me, too!"

"I'm not running out! Tell me what happened."

"All right. That dandy jigger — Colorado Jack, I think he's called — charged in like a thundergust. A madman, yellin' an' shootin' off two guns. The damn cows just jumped an' run with the horses. Lord knows what came of Jim Henry an' Half-star Ralph — they were riding herd. I stayed right here, under this wagon, me bein' no stupid hero!"

Mike gazed hopelessly around. In one stroke, Colorado Jack, rage-crazed, had wrecked everything. There wouldn't be a drive tonight, or any night in the foreseeable future. It would take many days to catch the horses and then round up the scattered herd. And the Middle Range cowmen, dead weary, were out of patience. They couldn't be goaded into the effort.

He pondered for a moment on Ould Burro's words of advice: *a deep seat in the saddle for a far destination.*

Escape from failure. Let others face the disaster, while he went on his way, free of it, to Mexico. Shuck it off and forget it. His gamble had gone bust. The cash stake was down the drain. Pull out.

He couldn't bring himself to do it. The reason for his reluctance, he told himself, was that he was tired of running. A wanted man had to make his final stand somewhere. This was as good a place as any for a man to face up to himself, face the consequences of misdeeds, failure.

Other riders dusted into camp: Middle Range cowmen, all raging mad. "Damn your triflin' soul to hell!" Peter Hardy rasped at Mike. "Colorado Jack stampeded our herd while you went skirtin' with the Brokus wench! He rode into Fifty and shouted it at us! Dared us to do something! We'd just got in from the Caven mess. My son got a gun and took him up on it. My son, Boy Pete! You taught him to use a gun, curse you!"

Mike winced, thinking of Boy Pete pitting his clumsy courage against Colorado Jack's expert technique. "Did he stroke, or did he dig at it?" he asked. But he knew the answer.

"You didn't teach him good enough!" said Ed Horner bitingly. "Colorado Jack shot him. First his wrist. And while Boy Pete stood there bleeding. Colorado Jack shot both his legs. And laughed at him falling! It's the only time I ever wished I was a damn gunman!"

"You've ruined my son! It never would've

happened 'cept for you! I'll curse you till my dying day, McLean! I wish I could do to you what's done to my boy!" Peter Hardy's voice shook, anguish quivering his lips. "My boy, my only son — broken and crippled! And no money left to bring in a doctor for him. Oh, God! What's to become of him?"

His work-gnarled hands clasped in prayerful supplication. "God, he don't deserve such punishment! He was a good boy. Let Thy wrath descend on the real sinner, this man who led him astray to violence!"

"Amen!" Ed Horner appended. "You led us to believe we could depend on you, McLean, an' you let us down! Herd an' remuda all scattered to blazes! We're wiped out worse off than before you came! You oughta be strung up!"

"In the name of God, no more violence this wicked night!" Peter Hardy proclaimed. "Don't stain your hands as his are stained!"

He wheeled his horse and rode off. The other cowmen followed more slowly, muttering in thin tones among themselves and casting glares back at Mike.

Crawling unsteadily out from his prudent retreat under the chuck wagon, Ould Burro observed, " 'Twould appear we're finished here, Michael! Methinks a quick vamoose is in order! Yon fellers are in an ugly mood."

Mike seated himself slumped on the wagon tongue. "Why wouldn't they be? Guess I'd feel the same way in their place. Hardy is right. A trouble maker, that's me. I'm a Jonah."

"Never mind the soul-searchin', Michael. Where do we go?" Ould Burro shook an empty bottle and sighed. "We've about run out of geography, dammit, an' it's a hard, dry road down to Mexico."

Mike slapped his hands on his knees. "Somehow I've got to raise cash." He stood up, wearily restless. "Got to!"

"A noble purpose," Ould Burro approved, perking up slightly. "I can't figger how ye'll go about it, our situation bein' as precarious as can be, but count me in."

"Not this time. It's for Boy Pete. He's got to have a doctor brought in to tend to him. Maybe hospital care, surgery, nurses. Albuquerque. The blame's mine that he got himself shot up — Hardy's right about that, too. I only see one way to get the cash, and you can't help."

"Ye sound mighty solemn, Mr. McLean, like a man on his way to the gallows!"

"That's how I feel, Mr. O'Burrifergus. Mighty solemn."

X
SACRIFICE

In the morning, after a sleepless night of long and bleak thoughts, Mike rode into the tiny town of Fifty, his decision unaltered.

Ould Burro insisted on going in with him, mentioning an urgent need of a drink to nail himself together, and adding pensively the information that he lacked the price. Mike had one last dollar, kept saved as a pocket-piece to guard off the bad-luck curse of being entirely broke. He gave it to Ould Burro, causing the old tinhorn to eye him searchingly before heading into the Log Cabin Bar. Ould Burro fully recognized the significance of parting with one's last coin.

Mike paid a call on the plain little paint-peeled Hardy house. Like a few other Middle Range cowmen who had known more prosperous years, Peter Hardy still lived in Fifty, running cattle on the open range where the working headquarters were mostly shacks.

Answering Mike's knock, Peter Hardy made to slam the door in his face at sight of him. Mike jammed a foot against it.

"Hold on a minute, Hardy! I've got something to say."

"I've got nothing to say to you, McLean, that can be said on a Sunday! Get your foot out!"

"Just give me a minute. You won't be sorry. How's Boy Pete? I've got to know."

Peter Hardy swung the door open, glowering with anger and grief. "So!" he spat bitterly. "You've got to know, do you? Why? What's it matter to you how he is?"

"I'm asking as a friend, offering help."

"A friend! Pah! What help? I'm tending to him best I know how, but he needs proper doctors. Surgeons. Hospital is where he should be."

"D'you reckon you could get him to Albuquerque in a spring wagon?"

"I'd be on the way with him now, if I had money to pay for —"

"All right, then," Mike said. "I'll tell you where to get the money. A thousand dollars."

He paused before taking the irrevocable step. The hot sun felt good. The surrounding rangeland and distant, blue-hazed mountains looked good to him. He would miss all that, in the close confinement of gray walls.

"I'm wanted for robbing a bank in Estancia," he said. "The banker, man named Drennan, posted a cash reward for my capture. Somebody'll earn it sooner or later. Let it be you, Hardy. We'll start north with Boy Pete in a wagon. You turn me in at Estancia, collect the reward, and take Pete on to the hospital in Albuquerque."

Peter Hardy's eyes flickered. "I took suspicion to you from the start. Your big Texas outfit's just wind. You're on the dodge. It don't surprise me — but this does! Why would a bank robber do it, give himself up? A trick?"

Mike gazed off at the far mountains. "No trick. It's not my trade, bank robbing. It wasn't smart to stick up Drennan in his bank, but I got mad. He caught me short on a note I owed for two thousand dollars. Refused to extend it, though he'd promised he would. He foreclosed. Took the small spread I'd slaved to build up, worth five thousand at bottom."

"That didn't justify armed robbery! Two wrongs don't make a right. You're by nature a man of violence."

"Don't blame nature for it. I learned it early. Anyway, I collected the difference from Drennan — three thousand — on my gun."

"Where did that money go? On riotous living?"

Mike shook his head wryly. "I didn't get to spend any of it. Got caught dead asleep outside Manzano by the town marshal and a band of armed citizens. Made a deal with the town marshal, same night. Cost me the three thousand to break jail, and at that he tried to shotgun me as I came out."

He abruptly changed the subject. "Get the wagon ready," he told Peter Hardy. "I'll be at the Log Cabin when you want me. Don't take too long. I might have a second thought about it and hit for Mexico, if you keep me waiting!"

"I'll get somebody to lend a hand. Boy Pete's bed will fit in the wagon, room to spare." Peter Hardy fumbled for further words. "Look," he began as Mike turned from him, "I don't know what to say. I don't hardly know what to think. I ain't been wrong about you. Not far wrong, by your own confession. But now —"

"We can talk on the road to Estancia."

Angling across the single street toward the Log Cabin Bar to bid Ould Burro goodbye, Mike slowed his stride to let a group of five incoming riders trot by. The five drew to a

119

halt, confronting him, and he came face to face with Roone.

He had never laid eyes on Amery Roone, and had only a sketchy description of him, but he knew immediately that this was the boss of Triangle T and head of the Regulators. It had to be. The man wore a stiff-brimmed hat, whipcord breeches, an Eastern-tailored coat. The four men behind him rode horses bearing the Triangle T brand. They were armed.

"You're McLean?"

It came as a snapped demand, rather than a query. There was sharpness in Amery Roone's eyes, a hard assurance in his manner. His coldly keen face, with beaked nose and thin lips, looked incapable of ever registering any emotion or human feeling, other than severity. To meet him was a shock, like meeting the speaking image of some cold-blooded tyrant from out of the past ages.

Mike nodded. "Yeah, I'm McLean." The man's very presence made his neck hairs bristle. "Guess you're Roone. What d'you want?"

Rarely had anyone addressed Mr. Amery Roone in that uncivil fashion. The four armed men, Regulators, narrowed their eyes at Mike. He studied them for intentions. If a gunfight had to come, let it come now while they sat mounted close together. Their horses would rear up with them, for sure, on the opening shot. His shot, first. At Roone. They knew it.

Roone chose to let the disrespect pass, although Mike got an impression that the frozen face masked anger. *A weakness in him*, Mike thought. *Can't stand a lack of humbleness on the part of lesser mortals. Might have guessed as much. Dig him there again.*

"I've heard of you, McLean," Roone commented in his clipped voice. "I'm told you broke a couple of my best men."

"They broke easy."

The four Regulators shifted restlessly, creaking their saddles. Roone glanced around at them and back at Mike. "You're well advised to leave this country!"

"My own advice," Mike said. "No say-so from you or anybody else."

Once more an impression of anger was concealed behind the mask. Contradicting the impression, however, Roone extended his right hand. "Good for you! I admire your independence. Shake!" False admiration. The lordly condescension prickled.

Yet to refuse the proffered hand would be loutish and petty. As he shook it briefly,

Mike was aware of Middle Range cowmen watching from windows and doorways along the street. The cowmen were sure to interpret his handshake with their enemy as an act of blatant treachery. And that, he realized tardily, was Roone's purpose.

"Hail and farewell, McLean!" Roone murmured mockingly. "You joined the wrong side! Where are you going from here?"

That, the out-of-line question on top of the Judas handshake, sparked Mike's temper. "Where I go is none of your goddamn business! I guess this country hasn't yet taught you right manners, among other things!"

An added pallor crept into the chill face. "Excuse me. I forgot for a minute the sensitive reactions of men who are on the wanted list. I'm not very familiar with the, hmm, etiquette of outlaws."

Roone touched up his horse. The four Regulators eyed Mike expressionlessly in passing. Mike proceeded on toward the Log Cabin Bar, not in an easy humor. This black day was going from bad to worse.

Predictably, into his path stepped several cowmen led by Ed Horner. He knew what was on their minds before they spoke. They planted themselves before him, barring him from stepping up onto the strip of broken boardwalk in front of the Log Cabin, so that he had to stand in the street.

"McLean! What's this between you 'n Roone?" Ed Horner moved his raw-boned frame closer to Mike. "We all saw you shake hands with him! Looks like you've sold out to Triangle T!"

Mike's hold on his temper slipped. "Well, you're wrong as usual! Don't pull that snuffy tone on me, Horner! I won't take it!"

Others came hurrying, slowing their pace when within earshot, loosely surrounding him. Some horsemen walked their horses briskly into town. He supposed they were Roone's Regulators returning to witness a promising brawl that had him on the short end. He didn't look around at them, but kept his eyes on Ed Horner.

The Middle Range cowmen were plainly on the prod, ready to pile into him if he gave them an opening. The gun he wore was all that deterred them. They must have stayed up all night, holding a stormy meeting, working themselves into an unreasoning rage. Disappointment and disaster had become unbearable. His handshake with Roone was the last straw.

He heard the horsemen halt directly behind him. Their silent presence there gave him cold creeps in the spine, and he snapped at Ed Horner and his group, "Out of my way! I'm in a hurry!"

One of the horsemen at his back drawled, "You *been* in a right smart hurry, McLean, but not as of now! Lift your hands up before you turn round, eh?"

That drawling voice, deceptively mild, was familiar to Mike. Turning slowly, empty hands raised, his first feeling was regret that the thousand dollar reward wouldn't go to Peter Hardy for Boy Pete's surgical care.

"Hello, Pringle," he said.

"Higher, McLean, pul-*ease!*" Sheriff George Pringle, of Estancia, spoke over a leveled gun. "Kindly pardon my insistence, but I know you too well to take a chance."

He was a veteran law officer who liked to affect an elaborate politeness, especially at critical moments. His long, sardonic face and disillusioned eyes gave him something of a sinister aspect, but it was on his record that he was as honest as a bloodhound and as stubborn in following the tracks of a fugitive.

Two part-time deputies, guns drawn, flanked the sheriff. They regarded Mike with grave detachment. He had been on good terms with them back in Estancia. As casual friends, they might personally have been glad if he had made good his getaway, he knew. As lawmen, though, they would strain the last notch to take him in. He knew that, too.

Still, it was some better than being taken by strangers. He raised his hands higher, as requested. " 'Lo, Bert. Hi, Webb. It's okay, Sheriff, I won't try anything on you. But I wish you'd got here a day later."

"Sorry it inconveniences you."

"It puts me in an embarrassing position. I promised a man my reward."

Pringle reached carefully and took Mike's gun from its holster. "Oh? You trying to tell me you aimed to give yourself up? You? Why?"

"I owe him a debt. That was the only way to pay it."

"Well, well! I could have a foolish inclination to believe you, maybe, only it's my recollection you departed Estancia with three thousand dollars!"

"I didn't keep it long."

"No?" Pringle squinted thoughtfully. "I think I can figure where it went. The Manzano jailbreak, eh? It smelled wrong to me when I got there next day. The town marshal seemed too perky, considering you'd busted his arm."

Mike didn't reply, reluctant to inform on

the Manzano marshal, although that crooked lawman had tried to doublecross and shotgun him in the fixed escape. Pringle nodded his understanding of the principle involved.

"There's no getting the money back now. Recovering it would've helped your case. Mr. Hebard Drennan's got more than a sentimental attachment for that money," the sheriff said with a strong tinge of irony. "There's been a run on his bank since you left. Estancia folks don't approve what you did, but they know why you did it. He's pressed for ready cash."

He jerked his head backward without taking his eyes off Mike. "Banker Drennan is about to become mighty sore at you, McLean!"

Mike looked past the sheriff and the two deputies. Down the street he saw Amery Roone and the Regulator squad returning into town. And alongside Roone rode Hebard Drennan, banker of Estancia, merchant and dealer in anything of value, sharp manipulator of mortgages and call-loans.

Everything was crowding in on him, everything coming at once, meshing together in a fatal pattern. Pringle smiled grimly at Mike's expression.

"Never rains but it pours, McLean!"

"That's a fact! But those two —"

"Business connections. Any banker's happy to do a dab of business for Triangle T. Mr. Roone keeps up with the news, I reckon, because he recognized your name and description, and sent word to Drennan you were here. You picked a tough hideout!"

"I was passing through," Mike said, "and got hung up in some trouble."

"H'm. Sounds like you," Pringle commented. "Drennan notified me. He came along to vouch for us, so we could slip in by way of Triangle T without somebody tipping you off. Also, of course, to recover his three thousand dollars. No, Mr. Drennan ain't going to be pleased! He'll be a vengeful citizen at your trial, demanding the full penalty of justice!"

"Thanks for the cheering words!"

XI
KNIVES IN THE DARK

The cowmen, edging nearer, had listened and looked on with growing amazement. "What's all this?" Ed Horner asked. "Are you honest-to-God lawmen? Are you arrestin' McLean?"

Sheriff George Pringle rested a solemn gaze on him. His years of experience had made him expert at gauging other men's moods, and he couldn't miss realizing that the temper of these men was ugly. His two deputies, catching it, sat motionless and stiff-faced, moving only their eyes.

The sheriff finally answered, "We are law officers making an arrest, as you have shrewdly guessed. Mr. McLean committed an unfortunate transgression. In an absent-minded moment he happened to rob a bank, for which misguided impulse he will probably be wearing white whiskers before he again walks free among free men." He was stringing out words to gain time. "The warrant for his arrest is in my pocket."

"What?" Ed Horner exclaimed. "Him rob a bank? Ain't he a big Texas cattleman?"

Pringle wagged his head sadly. "Mike McLean, you sure have gone bad! First it's bank robbery, then lying to these fine folks. You're on the downward road to perdition! To be any kind of cattleman means to own cattle. Which at the present time makes you totally not a cattleman!"

Ed Horner blared at McLean, "Why, you cussed four-flusher! You — you — !"

His fist caught Mike high on the cheek, a round-arm blow that knocked Mike stumbling sideways away from his captors. Instantly, the crowd went beserk.

"Whoa, there!" Pringle rapped, taken aback. "Whoa, you bronc-heads! Lay off my prisoner!"

He had handled threatening mobs before, and had estimated these people at about average. Ordinarily fair and moderate, for them to attack a disarmed prisoner was to flout their common principles of decent behavior.

Principles fled. The final exposure of Mike McLean as a penniless outlaw and impostor was too much. The cowmen rushed at him. It flashed through his mind, ironically, that he, who had strived to arouse their fighting spirit, was the victim of his own teachings. Disregarding the lawmen's brandished guns and plunging horses, they swamped him, all out to get in a lick and tear him apart. Their voices swelled to a roaring chant.

"Get him! Get him . . ."

Using fists, elbows, boots, Mike fought to his feet. Some enraged rioter hurled a hammer at his head from the open door of the blacksmith shed. He saw it coming, ducked, tried to catch it for a weapon, and a heavy clout sent him floundering. He bounded up again and belted Ed Horner in the jaw, and butted down two men in a headlong break to the Log Cabin.

He got his back against the saloon front, slamming his fists and boots at all comers. Faces before him swirled contorted, snarling, unrecognizable as the faces of men he had ridden and worked with during the roundup.

Sheriff Pringle and his two deputies vainly attempted to force their horses into the packed crowd, to rescue their prisoner. Knowing little of the cause, they were at a loss to account for the furious flare-up. Its suddenness had caught them by surprise, and they weren't quite prepared to cope with it.

Amery Roone and his party rode up,

halted in the street, and sat looking on at the riot, making no move to interfere. The banker, Drennan, baggy eyes bulging with alarm, said something to Roone, who smiled frostily and shook his head.

Ould Burro barged out of the Log Cabin, derringer in one hand, the barman's bung-starter in the other. "Hold the fort, Michael, I'm coming!" he clarioned. Somebody fetched him a terrific smack and he took a backward header into the barroom and stayed there.

Mike landed his fist on a sparring, weaving cowman, and teetered against the saloon front for balance. He crouched, as mad now as any of them, glaring through his tumbled hair. He butted a charging man in the middle and kicked the feet out from under another.

"Fight, is it?" he grated. "You goddamn forty-to-one warriors, I'll give you a fight!" In a springing start from the saloon front, he dived into the thick of them.

The dust-hung air was full of fists and feet. He toppled three men to the ground with him, reared up with another clinging to his back, jackknifed and sent that encumbrance flying overhead, and dived in again.

They didn't give way. They tore into him like hounds at a cornered panther. The thud of blows given and taken beat a broken tattoo to their grunting. His face and knuckles bloody, he smashed on, hoping they might fall back if he forced the damage. He took a punch that rang bells in his head. Recovering dizzily, spraddle-legged, he handed one back to the giver and drove him colliding into those clamoring behind.

Someone on the ground clutched hold of his legs. He tried to kick loose. A fist got through his flailing arms and rocked him badly. He struck out awkwardly while making the effort to keep his footing. If he went down now, it was farewell.

Down he fell, slammed off balance, landing on top of the man clutching his legs. The man let go, scrambling to get clear of the boots that were closing in, and some of the foremost men pressed back to make way for him. In the cramped space left, Mike fought to his feet.

Sheriff Pringle gave up trying to reach Mike. Angry, he called, "McLean, here's your gun! Catch!" He tossed it over the heads of the crowd.

Mike caught the gun by its barrel. He rammed the butt at the forehead of a man who sprang to grab for it. He flipped the gun over in his hand and triggered two shots, not caring much where the bullets went.

A shot cracked from a different gun, then another and another. Horsemen, a solid column of them, came plowing into the crowd; hard-faced men who stuck their spurred boots out wickedly in the stirrups as they forced through, reckless of how many respectable citizens got hurt. They smiled, booting men out of their way, splitting the crowd apart.

The cowmen around Mike fell back. Cut and bruised, one eye puffed shut, he slashed his gunbarrel at them. Half blinded, he stumbled off the edge of the boardwalk and righted himself to meet the mounted newcomers. With his good eye he then saw the leading rider of the column.

The Cheyenne Flame kept an easy seat in the saddle of her nervously dancing horse. Reins wrapped over her forearm, she reloaded a smoking gun. She wore her range garb and wide sombrero. Back of her rode Bloody-wire Charley Brokus and his wild Alta Mesa bunch.

Brokus bellowed a huge laugh, reining in. "As grand a scrap as I've seen since Montana Monte took on the crowd at Trinidad, rest his sinful soul! They make men yet, hell if they don't! McLean, you revive my faith in human nature! She" — he jutted his beard at Flame — "was for buttin' in sooner. Likes your style. So do I. But I wouldn't bust up good fun. Ah, to be young again! Man your face is a mess!"

He waved a hand imperiously at the Middle Range cowmen. "Move, you psalm-singin' nursemaids! *Vamoose!*" His eyes, sweeping over Sheriff George Pringle and the two deputies, sharpened, and abruptly his manner changed. "Lawmen! You don't belong here!"

"We came in on Mr. Roone's word," Pringle said quietly.

Mike trudged unsteadily to him. "Here's my gun back. Thanks for throwing it to me."

Pringle took the gun. "I couldn't let 'em beat you to death, could I?" he asked almost defensively. "You didn't take advantage an' turn the gun on me."

"Doubt if my aim's any good right now."

"You'd have tried if you wanted. It won't make me happy taking you to jail, tell you that."

"Jail for what?" demanded Brokus.

"Bank robbery. That there's the banker," Pringle nodded his head toward Drennan. "Three thousand dollars taken, an' McLean lost it all in a jailbreak. I'm George Pringle, sheriff from Estancia."

"And I'm Charley Brokus, boss of Alta Mesa. I've got twenty-odd men with me. You don't take anybody! It'd set a bad example here!"

"The sheriff's a kind of friend of mine," Mike said. "So're Bert and Webb."

Brokus quirked an eyebrow. "What's that mean?"

"Means I wouldn't want 'em killed on my account."

"Tough. You don't make things easy on y'self, do you, McLean?" Brokus grinned, a curious gleam in his eyes. He swung around and called, "Mr. Roone. We meet today to make our peace an' bury the hatchet, right?"

"Right, Mr. Brokus," replied Roone. "Sorry for the trouble at the *baile*. A misunderstanding."

"Sure. Let bygones be bygones. Have you got anything against McLean that you can't overlook?"

"Well, no, if you —"

"*Bueno!* I wouldn't want us to quarrel, Mr. Roone." The congenial formality between them sounded ludicrous, after their long and bitter enmity. "Then it's okay with you if I pull him out of his jackpot?"

"With me, yes. However, Mr. Drennan here is a banker who has —"

"His bank got took for three thousand

dollars, this lawman says," Brokus interrupted. He glanced at Colorado Jack sitting his horse besides him. "Only three thousand. Would we let a good man rot in jail for that? Not me!"

His hand snapped on Colorado Jack's wrist, a lightning stroke, twisting the arm back with powerful ease. None of his men moved. His daughter only glanced at him.

"Not me!" Brokus repeated, retaining his grip. "But we'll settle one thing at a time, if you please. My *caporal* itches for McLean's blood, I notice! It makes me wonder why." He tightened his grip. "Why, Col? I'll bust your arm! What's he done to bristle you? Tell me!"

"I'll tell you," Mike said. "It's what *he's* done. Last night he stampeded the herd, then gunned down a friend o' mine."

"Ah!" breathed Brokus, not sure that he had unearthed the root of the matter. "So you did it, Col — did what you wanted! Not on my order, goddamn you! I got a mind to let McLean have you for that!"

Colorado Jack turned his head to Flame, who was looking at Mike. His eyes flared. "It'd suit me! Guns, knives, fists — anything! Damn right I itch for his blood!"

"Turn him loose," Mike said, "and I'll take him on!"

Brokus guffawed his huge laugh, pleased to bring the matter down to raw violence. "Two devil-be-damned scrappers, eh? Spoilin' for a fight! I'm all for it. Shape you're in, McLean, you couldn't hit a barn, though, an' Col's a dead shot. Well, there's an answer to everything."

He gestured to his Alta Mesa men; they came instantly alert, awaiting his order.

"Put 'em both in the blacksmith shed," he told them. "Take Col's guns off him. Let 'em keep their knives. Shut the doors. No light. How's that for an even break, McLean? You won't need eyes in the dark."

"It'll do, I guess, if you say so."

"I say so! Be it done! A fairly even match, don't you think, Mr. Roone?" Brokus shrugged off Flame's urgently whispered protests. "Sure, McLean's bunged-up. He can still fight!"

"An equable arrangement, yes," Roone agreed, pulling at his necktie and bowing to Flame. "Some of my men would welcome the chance to take your man's place. My foreman got shot at the dance. By McLean, I'm told."

"Sorry. Boys will be boys, Mr. Roone."

"McLean isn't a boy!"

"True, true. He's quite a man." Again the curious gleam flickered in Brokus' eyes. A

gleam of cynical cunning and crafty cogita-
tion. The king of Alta Mesa didn't rule by
brute force alone. "I can use him," he muttered.

"What?"

"Nothing."

The eyes of the two leaders met, friendly
on the surface, utterly faithless beneath.

Mike felt for his knife in his pants pocket, a
cowman's ordinary pocket jackknife, not
designed for combat. Colorado Jack had a
bowie sheathed on his belt, its heavy blade
sized to castrate a grown bull or carve it up
for beef. He most likely knew how to throw
it and hit an inch of target, in which case
the match was nowhere near even.

They stepped into the blacksmith shed.
Colorado Jack paced to the far side and
stood there, back to the wall, eyes roving,
mapping obstructions, memorizing them
while the light allowed him. He was a cool,
planning killer now, not a maniac. Mike
heard Brokus calling out, "Anybody want to
lay a bet who comes out o' the shed alive?
Name your fancy!"

"What odds?"

"No odds. Even money."

"Fifty on Jack!"

"A hunerd, here!"

"Taken!" said Brokus. "Any others? Come on, faint heart never won fair lady! Mr. Roone?"

"I never gamble, Mr. Brokus."

The double doors of the blacksmith shed banged shut. There were no windows. As the daylight blacked out, Mike heard Colorado Jack's swift shift of position. He sank to a squat.

Iron tongs whammed the wall behind him and clanged on the earthen floor. Colorado Jack wasn't limiting himself to his bowie knife. The knife was for the sure-death thrust. The dark shed was rich in potential weapons, missiles. Mike stayed motionless, guarding his breath.

"Mr. Brokus!" he heard Pringle say edgily. "You sure take high-handed liberties with my prisoner!"

"Prisoner, hell!" retorted Brokus. "You only take him if he's dead!"

Mike silently cursed Brokus for setting up this creeping duel in the dark. It wasn't his kind of fighting and he had no liking for it. His good eye was watering, closing. The sun-warped planks of the blacksmith shed were sure to let in cracks of daylight here and there, but he couldn't see them. He remembered that Colorado Jack had cat's eyes.

XII
BOUGHT AND PAID
FOR

Minutes passed. Reason warned him to stay where he was, quiet and unmoving. He had to depend on his ears and listen for Colorado Jack to make a sound. But instinct prodded him to shift. Or was it, he thought, the impatience of strained nerves? To play a waiting game had never held much appeal for him.

He left his position and began edging around the shed in a blind search for Colorado Jack. He wished he'd been able to fix in his mind the contents and layout of the shed before the doors closed. Colorado Jack had surely done so, and now he was soundlessly stalking, no question of that, for neither did he have the temperament for a waiting game.

Mike's head brushed against something dangling from a rafter, and instinctively he ducked low from it. It swung in the darkness, then let out the soft clang of an iron wagon-wheel lightly striking wood. An instant, single thud, above and just behind him, puzzled Mike momentarily. He reached up. His fingers came in contact with the handle of a knife, its blade driven deep into the plank wall.

"Lost your bowie!" he said. It had been a lightning throw of terrific force, the aim and range deadly accurate except that he had ducked his head just before the wagon-wheel clanged.

"It was worth tryin'!" came the whispered reply. "Now shuck your blade, if you're a fightin' man, an let's slog this out even! Barehanded, no irons?"

"You bet!" Mike tossed away his knife, stepping forward, abandoning stealth. His ears caught a faint sound, a tiny, muffled click. "Where are you?"

"Right here!" Colorado Jack's voice crooned a fierce mirth. "An' comin' right up!"

Mike spun half around. Knuckles scraped his face. He sucked a breath in sudden, smarting pain, his chest blade-ripped by a slash that was meant for his neck. It hadn't occurred to him that Colorado Jack carried a clasp knife as well as the bowie.

He jumped back to avoid the next slash, and the backs of his legs collided with the anvil block. He toppled onto the anvil, rolled over it, and fetched up sprawled across the blacksmith's open-head water barrel. The smithy had the usual habit of hanging all his variously shaped tongs on the lip of the barrel, a dozen or more. It felt like tumbling into a pitfall of iron stakes.

The jangling clatter brought a laugh from the dark. "Howya doin', McLean? I'm gonna cut off your head an' kick it out the door!"

Falling off the water barrel, Mike dragged loose a pair of two-foot tongs weighing ten pounds and let fly, much too high. They hit a rafter of the low roof, but evidently fell down on Colorado Jack, judging from his change of language. Mike flung another pair in the direction of the muttered curse. He kept on hurling tongs until the supply ran out, and sailed the blacksmith's hammers after them. Locating a pile of horseshoe blanks alongside the forge, he renewed the bombardment, pitching them in every direction he judged likely to score results.

Outside, Brokus boomed, "How can two men raise that much racket? If I didn't know, I'd swear it was forty broncs an' a bear in there! Any more bets?"

It wasn't possible for Mike to estimate his score, but a couple of times he heard a gasped oath. He had hit about everything inside the shed, and by the law of averages he should have banged the target, he guessed. Colorado Jack was holding off, perhaps only waiting to get in his work with his clasp knife after the missiles ceased crashing around.

Getting down to the last horseshoe blank in the pile, Mike gripped the rough-wrought iron in his fist, reserving it as a weapon. He wiped his streaming eye on his shirtsleeve and went prowling for Colorado Jack. Not finding him, he stood still, listening. He could hear nothing except the rumbling voices outside, but his senses shrilled warning of a living presence, of eyes watching him. He thumbed a match alight and held it overhead.

Colorado Jack stood crouched against a wall of the shed. His right arm dangled, the shoulder lower than the other. One side of his face was a raw mass, bleeding. He had been holding his breath, waiting in utter silence for Mike to draw near.

They glared at each other under the light of the upheld match, a distance of three paces between them. Letting his breath out shudderingly, Colorado Jack lurched forward, the clasp knife in his left hand sweeping at Mike's neck.

Mike pulled back, sidestepped, and hit him one blow with the horseshoe as he floundered by on buckling legs. The match burned Mike's fingers and he dropped it.

He couldn't find the doors in the dark, and called hoarsely, "Open up, you out there!"

They opened up, giving light, and he made himself walk straight out. He was shaking all through, wracked with pain, a gory hobgoblin in tatters. He peered at misty shapes of men, dully hating them.

"Go carry your *caporal* out!" he told them. "I don't think he's dead, but he sure can't walk!"

"Pay me, boys, pay me!" Brokus roared hilariously. "My money was on you, McLean! What made all the racket in there?"

"Pitching horseshoes," Mike said. The crowd was blurring worse. He had difficulty keeping upright. "I hung ringers on him." He hated Brokus then, too, for putting him through the savage ordeal; for using him to win bets.

Brokus slapped his thigh, laughing. "Hung ringers on Col, he says. Can't hardly see or stand up, but he can still crack a joke! Haw! Sheriff, what's he worth?"

Sheriff George Pringle fingered his chin, scanning Mike reflectively. "He took three thousand dollars from the bank. The only actual witness is Mr. Drennan, victim of the holdup. If McLean had the money to give back, I think Mr. Drennan might be persuaded to, er, mistrust his recollection of who took it."

"Yeah," said Brokus. "How 'bout you?"

"I'd be satisfied in that case." Pringle coughed gently. "It's a fair piece back to Estancia. End of a day's tiring ride, I might absentmindedly start a fire with the warrant. No arrest, no trial, file closed."

"You're one of the rare old stock, Sheriff, broad-minded an' reasonable," Brokus complimented him grandly. "You know you can't take McLean long's I don't want him took anyway."

"The weight of the majority is on your side, I grant."

The look in Brokus' eyes was granite hard, calculating. "I'll foot his bill to the banker. D'you hear me, McLean, or are you as fogged as you look? I'm payin' three thousand cash for you!"

Mike was fogged, but a thought stuck in his head. "Make it four thousand," he said. "A thousand to me." He wiped a hand down his chest, smearing the drying, gritty blood of the knife wound. Black numbness rose in slow, sickening waves.

Brokus chuckled. "Can still drive a bargain, too, eh? Four thousand it is — on my terms, which you've got to agree to first."

"What terms?"

"I want your word you'll pay off your debt to me by workin' for me. Means you'll take my orders, no questions, no argument! An', let's see" — Brokus blinked thoughtfully up at the sky — "you'll swear to guard the interests o' me an' mine at any cost, so help you God!" Incongruous words, coming from him.

"Give my word," Mike mumbled. "S' help me God . . ."

He missed a clutch at the blacksmith's open door and keeled over. The last he heard was Sheriff Pringle, bent above him, muttering, "Did what I could for you, but I've sure got misgivings about it. Crafty old wolf's tied you tight to him, body and soul. Jail might've been better. . . ."

The Brokus house up on Alta Mesa was a sprawling adobe structure ungraced by any style of design, a mud mansion rising three floors high at one end and tapering off from there to a hodgepodge of added-on rooms and wings. Its outer walls, thick as the walls of a fortress, kept the interior cool on the hottest day of summer. The small windows, deeply recessed, had shutters.

Here and there in angles of the building were odd-shaped little *placitas* that, in the Spanish Southwest fashion, should have contained flowers, but didn't. This was predominantly a habitation of men. There were limits to what one girl, Flame, could accomplish with such an immense household, helped only by transient women who never stayed long.

Mainly a headquarters, the place had spread haphazardly out through the years as Brokus' crew increased and his prosperity grew. No bunkhouse, though. No cook shack. Self-containment was the keynote. The men's quarters were in a long wing of the house, and everyone ate in a barren great room, at hand-hewn log tables so heavy they would have required a team of oxen to drag. They ate anything served them, usually cursing the cook, but there was always plenty of it and they'd do worse elsewhere. Jail grub. No pay.

An outlaw roost.

Yet it was restful to lounge lazing in the shaded side of a flagstoned *portico,* cool water in an Indian clay *olla* hanging within reach, smoking, gazing out over the plain below. The Brokus range lay east of the mesa. It was over-grazed, weedy, showing

147

bald expanses of bare earth. The outfit ran a large herd on it, besides using it as a stopover for hard-driven cattle mostly from Texas and Mexico.

The overgrazing created a problem. Brokus would have to trim down the size of his herd, or curtail his raiding forays. Or, more his roughshod style, Mike reflected, grab more range and spread out. Bigness imposed a penalty upon itself. It couldn't stand still. The more a man possessed, the more he wanted. Brokus could never re-trench, trim his herd, pay off half of the oversize crew, and live on his gains. He had to go on winning more, never satisfied.

"So you and Triangle T are burying the hatchet," Mike commented as Brokus joined him on the *portico.* "Burying it in whose skull?"

Brokus grinned, lighting a cigar. He hooked a chair into the shade and sat down. "Our meetin' bore ripe fruit. I told Roone the trouble between us was my blame. Just a sorry ol' fool, me. 'Mr. Brokus —' says he, to which I said, 'Call me Charley.' To which *he* said, 'Much of the blame for it is on my side, Charley. Call me Amery.' That was real big of him, wasn't it?"

"Big of you, too."

"Sure. In that happy light o' friendship

an' trust, we made a deal. I get a free hand to rid the Middle Range o' them pesky cow-squatters, Hardy an' them. That's where the hatchet goes! Then me an' Roone share the whole Llano, open range, good neighbors, standin' together against anybody outside tryin' to move in. We shook hands on it. United we stand! *Bueno,* eh?"

Yawning, Mike stretched cautiously. The knife-slash across his chest was about healed, but too-energetic movements twinged reminders of it. His face was almost back to normal.

"Bueno," he said, "like dreams of gold!"

Brokus eyed him blandly. "Roone's dreams, not mine! Speakin' o' gold, what did you do with the thousand dollars I gave you?"

"Loaned me. To be worked off at high interest, I suspect."

"Right! Did it go with your Irish tramp, on the trip to Fifty you sent him yest'day?"

"It went to pay a man what I promised. What I owed him."

"You don't welsh on your debts, McLean! I knew it. You're one o' the —"

"Save the salve! You put up four thousand dollars on my word." Mike changed the subject, saying, "I can't see you and Roone

149

pulling together. You don't match. You'll split."

"No," Brokus said, "Roone swallered the bait. Won't give us much trouble to land him." He paused. "Who's trying to sing in there? Your tinhorn?"

Mike nodded. "Mr. Timothy Sean Mario O'Burrifergus, known as Ould Burro, is drunk. I'm not sure you did right, bringing him here along with me. You should keep your whiskey locked up, anyway."

"He ain't no prize," Brokus agreed carelessly, "but he's an amusin' ol' cuss. I might make him my court jester, like Flame says kings useta have. I'm king here, begod!"

Mike bowed in his chair without rising. "King Charles, emperor of Alta Mesa! May I ask your royal highness how the hell you baited Roone into making a deal with you?"

"Trappin' was my trade, long time back. I can bait a coyote! Y'know, you're an amusin' cuss, too, in a diff'rent way. Glad I got you. This place —"

"What bait did you use on Roone?"

Brokus spat a flake of leaf tobacco, frowning at the wet end of his cigar. "Flame," he said.

Mike shot up from his chair. "You bastard!"

"Careful, McLean — careful!" A fast-

150

drawn gun covered him. Brokus had fore-seen his reaction and was ready for it. "Sit down! You'll have jumpin' a-plenty to do next Sunday. Roone's had an eye for Flame these two years past. I'm not blind to him. Not blind to you, either!"

"Your own daughter, you —"

"I didn't pay four thousand dollars for your lip! Shut up an' listen!" The iron was in Brokus' harsh command. "You swore to take my orders, remember, an' guard the interests o' me an' mine at any cost! No questions, no argument!"

He leaned back, nodding, as Mike slowly sank into his chair. "Sunday's the day. A quiet weddin'. I wanted to have it here, o'course, but Roone was cagey, so we settled on havin' it at his place. It'll be, he said, a fortunate union of two great houses previously at war. The smooth talk o' the man! The —"

"How about Flame?" Mike broke in. "How does she feel about marrying him?"

"She'll do what I think's best. Flame's a good girl. I'm mighty fond of her."

"Looks like it! You're selling her for —"

"Hobble your tongue an' pay 'tention. For some legal reason, Triangle T is held in Roone's name. Maybe the Eastern owners find it convenient to keep their names off the record. Now, in this country a widow inherits her dead husband's property. All right. Sunday afternoon, Flame becomes the lawful wedded wife of Amery Roone. Right after the weddin', a fatal misfortune makes her his widow — legal owner o' Triangle T!"

Mike blinked at the murderous treachery of the scheme. "What about the Eastern owners — the real owners?"

"To hell with 'em! We'll take over long before they can make any move. Possession's nine points o' the law. It's all ten points here!"

Clenching his fingers, Mike hunched forward. "That inheritance law works both ways. If *she* dies, he gets *her* property, including what she's inherited from her father — who could become her late lamented father damned sudden if he don't watch sharp!"

Brokus flapped a hand. "You're way behind me! That's an extra bait I used on Roone. He'll try a whizzer if he sees a chance, sure, but I'm too fast for him. I'll be cattle king o' the whole Llano, an' my daughter'll be cattle princess!"

"You're gambling her life as well as your own!" Mike accused him. "Roone's no fool. He's liable to outsmart you."

"What?" Brokus flung up his massive, bearded head. "I can beat any man at any game!"

"He's got his Regulators, don't forget."

"An' I've got my crew. We'll all be at the weddin'. My daughter'll be safe. I'll have the right man planted there to gun down Roone first off, at my signal."

"A reliable man?" Mike queried.

"I think he is," returned Brokus blandly, "or I sure wouldn'ta paid four thousand dollars for him!"

"You're asking me to murder Roone?"

"Askin' you nothin'. It's an order! Who else would I pick to make sure Flame's a widow? I don't want it botched. I'd as soon see her dead as livin' with Roone."

"So would I, but —"

"That's what I figgered. So you've got a big job comin' up Sunday, guardin' the interests o' me an' mine! At any cost! Like you swore on your oath you'd do! I'm dependin' on you." Brokus got to his feet. His cigar had gone out, and he dropped it. In a tone less harsh, he said, "Don't let Flame down."

"Does she know?" Mike asked.

"About the setup?" Brokus shook his head. "I ain't told her, but she likely guesses I've got a trick up my sleeve. She knows me. Knows I wouldn't marry her off to that fish for keeps. Don't you let her down."

XIII
TRIANGLE T

The grave voice of the preacher from Alamogordo droned out through the open windows: "Repeat after me. *I take this man . . .*"

It was the only definite sound in the hot, quiet Sunday afternoon. In the wide yard the two separate groups of men idly watched white-coated Mexican servants scurrying with last preparations for the wedding feast spread on the Triangle T lawn.

Roone's house, nothing like the adobe mansion on Alta Mesa, had been planned by an architect from the East; it looked as civilized as a hearse.

Perhaps it was the bride who set the somber cloud over this wedding. Unsmiling, eyes haunted, she had entered the house, still alone among men, pale with foreboding like a virgin led to sacrifice in some barbaric rite that was disguised under elegant trappings. The men in the yard listened to the ending lines of the marriage service.

"Whom God hath joined . . ."

There was no mixing between the two groups. It was natural and to be expected that the Regulators, Triangle T hands, should congregate close to the long bunkhouse, clannish and stiffly reserved in the presence of old enemies. It was just as natural for the Alta Mesa men to clot together in the shade of the wagon shed. Brokus had foreseen it and fitted his plan to that arrangement.

Guns hidden under clean shirts and jackets, their horses within easy distance behind the wagon shed, the Alta Mesa men waited. They knew what they were here to do and how much Brokus would pay them for doing it. His plan had a forthright, simple ruthlessness that appealed to their reckless inclinations. Smash Triangle T at one stroke.

First, the shot at Roone. That was Mike McLean's task, to gun him down the instant Brokus gave the signal. In the flare-up, Brokus would get his daughter safely away from the house. The rest would be up to his crew, ramrodded by Mike. Take over the outfit then and there, in the interests of its new young mistress, at gunpoint. If they couldn't make it stick, if the coup went bad, jump for the horses and get gone.

Either way, it would work out in the end, because Roone would be dead. The Regulators wouldn't stay around to fight for a dead boss, no more pay forthcoming. They'd pull out, and Brokus would move in, king of the Llano.

Mike had no stomach for his part in it — to drop Roone with the opening shot and free the bride, make her a widow before she was a bedded wife. As long as he thought of Flame, the pawn in the murderous game, he could hold steady to his purpose. It had to be done, for her sake — and he knew very well that Brokus was banking on just that. That scheming old robber had him weighed and figured, and — as Sheriff Pringle had said — tied tight to him.

As the father of the unblushing bride, Brokus was an honored wedding guest in the Roone house, dressed for it. He exuded magnificent dignity along with kindly benevolence. An indulgent father, proud of his grown-up little girl.

Colorado Jack had insisted on coming along with the Alta Mesa bunch. The effort of riding broke out sweat on him. He was a changed man, once-handsome face misshapen, eyes sunken, his shoulder and arm bulkily bandaged in a sling.

Nobody in the Alta Mesa crew paid him attention. He had been *caporal*, but in jungle law the defeated went into the discard. Mike McLean now was the acknowledged ramrod, gun boss of the crew, even if the job didn't suit his wishes.

The voice of the preacher ceased in the house. Others replaced it, topped by Brokus' booming congratulations and good wishes. The ceremony was ended. Amery Roone and Flame Brokus were man and wife till death did them part, and next in order came the joyous celebration, the convivial gathering of everyone at the wedding feast. All was ready. There was a wedding cake to be cut by the bride.

"They'll come out in a minute, eh, McLean?" Colorado Jack whispered through chattering teeth. "All eyes on the front door, eh?"

"Man, how you shake!" The broken gun boss was running a fever, Mike reckoned. "You better slip off before it starts." This wasn't going to be any place for a sick man whose nerves had gone ragged.

Colorado Jack nodded, seemingly relieved, and limped into the wagon shed. It had a rear door by which he could get to his horse without drawing notice.

"Act natural," Mike murmured to the Alta Mesa men. They stood too tensely poised. "Roone's crew is watching us. You don't show a gun till I shoot, remember. And I don't shoot till Brokus gives the nod. Here he comes now."

It failed to relax them. Colorado Jack's whispered caution had tightened them up. They knew Roone's men were watching them closely, openly staring as if challenging their ability to spring a surprise.

Brokus emerged from the house, magnificently clad in gray trousers, frock coat, white shirt and silk necktie. Smiling, the picture of a proud father well satisfied with his daughter's marriage, he didn't betray the slightest sign of nerves. Hell was set to break loose on his signal, but he acted perfectly at ease.

Lighting a cigar, he beamed at the laden tables on the lawn. "Amery," he called over his shoulder, "you sure do things up grand! My, my, do I see champagne? Haven't tasted it since I was in 'Frisco. Come on, bring Flame out an' we'll pop the first bottle. Let's have a toast to your long an' happy future!"

"Of course, Charley, of course!" responded the cool, clipped voice of Amery Roone from within the house. "Nothing will please me more."

"Nor me!"

But nobody came out after Brokus. He stood on the edge of the lawn and puffed at his cigar, gazing ponderingly at the champagne bottles. From the house came a small sound like a muffled cry. Brokus turned, looking back inquiringly. He frowned slightly and glanced toward the Triangle T men in front of the long bunkhouse. The cigar in his teeth went motionless.

Preoccupied with the secret humor of his hypocrisy, he had missed sensing the strained tension in the yard. He sensed it now. His gaze flicked to the wagon shed. His face froze. The amiable pose dropped from him and on the instant he was again old Bloody-wire Brokus, veteran badman. He stabbed a hand under his frock coat to the armpit.

A shot whanged loudly inside the wagon shed. Brokus frowned deeper, finished his armpit draw, and fired. A sobbing sigh joined the ringing echoes in the shed. Mike spun around and saw Colorado Jack falling out of a buggy, his gun trailing a wisp of smoke.

A burst of rapid gunfire shattered the remaining hush of the Sunday afternoon. In the house, Roone called, "A toast, Charley!

160

A toast to your short and dismal future!"

The yard was a death trap, a bullet-swept execution ground. Roone's men, too, knew what they were there to do. On the cue of Colorado Jack's shot at Brokus, they had dropped to the ground and opened fire. At the same time, half a dozen riflemen got into sniping action from the upstairs windows of the house.

An Alta Mesa man fell heavily against Mike, coughing curses. Mike shoved him off, slung two shots low at the prone gunners, and backed into the wagon shed. Others dived in after him, shaken by the blazing onslaught, seeking any cover they could find. This thing had gone bad.

Brokus, his white shirt blotched red, shouted, "Get to the horses!" He lumbered across the yard, fell to his knees and rose unsteadily. "McLean!"

Mike ran out to him, swearing at him. The yard was a shambles of dead and wounded men, the white-clothed tables on the green lawn a mockery.

Men who had made it into the wagon shed piled on out through its rear door. They didn't panic, being what they were, killer gunmen, but they recognized this as a disastrous jackpot. They jumped for their horses behind the wagon shed, every man for himself, the devil take care of anyone electing to stand and get himself slain.

Roone's men, at the bunkhouse, promptly sprang up and cut around the wagon shed, firing mercilessly. They were drilled to kill the Alta Mesa guests. This was their home ground, and they knew every inch of it. The riflemen at the upstairs windows sniped shots at the wounded, at any enemy movement that was visible to them.

Brokus, falling again, bumped into Mike and hung onto him. "It's a *'buscado,* be-god!"

"Yeah! He outsmarted you!" Mike dragged him into the wagon shed, bullets flailing the ground behind them.

A tough grin. "We still got a chance, boy, long's the horses ain't spooked off! Never say die! We'll come back an' show them jiggers a fight that'll curdle 'em!" Brokus still believed he was indefeatable — with Colorado Jack's bullet lodged in his chest and his wild bunch scamping out of the slaughter. "Get to home, boys!" he roared, then spat a glob of blood. "Christ! The son-of-a-bitch sure hit me!"

The horses danced, reared, some breaking their bridle-reins and bolting off. Rifle fire continued relentlessly from the upstairs window of the house, picking off men running after their horses. A massacre.

Mike straight-armed a man and took his horse from him. He rode down and captured a runaway, and circled back with it to Brokus, "Climb on, smart guy, quick!"

A rifle bullet whipped off his hat. He fired at the upstairs windows. "Let's go!" Another bullet thunked into Brokus, legging onto the saddle. Sighing, Brokus righted himself.

The surviving men of the Alta Mesa crew streamed off headlong down the ranch road, riding bent low and lashing their horses. For a minute it looked like a getaway for them. Then the brush along both sides of the road burst noisily alive, gunfire spurting at near pointblank range, and horses and men spilled as if on trip-wires. Roone hadn't overlooked anything in his plan for an efficient wipe-out.

Brokus reined his horse hard over, holding it back from racing onward after the others into the ambush. " *'Buscado!* Look at 'em go down! Satan's sins, what next!" He swayed and jolted clumsily in the saddle, his horse dancing in circles. "Hey, I got trouble stayin' on this nag!"

"Too bad!" Mike spurred past him off the ranch road. "I'm cutting for those hills. Hang on and follow!"

■ ■ ■ ■

Darkening the earth, changing the hills to blue-black silhouettes streaked with red crinkles, sundown at last masked hunted from hunters and ushered in the quiet evening. A coyote howled its false mourning, ending in sharp yaps, summoning its kind to the hungry business of the night. Somewhere far off a bull bellowed mighty challenge to any other bulls that might be pawing around.

Bloody-wire Charley Brokus was dying.

"I should've figgered Col would sell us out," he said, "after you busted him an' I made you *caporal*. He had a gun lined on your back for his first shot, till he saw me dig for mine. They were ready, all set to go." He rasped a rattling breath. "My oath, we took a lickin' this day, didn't we? That tricky Roone!"

"Yeah, they beat us to it," Mike said.

They lay in an arroyo, their horses drooping nearby, Brokus' saddle blood-caked. Brokus stretched out, his boots scraping the sandy bed of the dry arroyo.

"In my time I've outsmarted an' outfought a score the likes o' Roone. Must be I'm gettin' old. Guess I'm through. It's up to you

164

now, McLean."

"What is?" Mike asked absently, his thoughts elsewhere.

"To get my daughter outa that jam, of course! Dammit, listen!" Brokus' eyes narrowed. His brain still worked. "She won't be at Triangle T tonight, not if I know Roone. He'll take over Alta Mesa right off quick an' make sure. We only left three men there, countin' your Burro tinhorn."

"You think Roone will want Flame there with him?"

"He sure will! To show her he's boss. Humble her. Make a slave o' my daughter in her own home. Besides, he'll figger to use her for bait to draw me out o' hidin'. He knows I'm hit, but not how bad. You get her out, hear?"

"How?"

"How the goddamn do I know? You do it, that's all!" Brokus stared up at Mike. "It's an order!"

"I don't need any order for that," Mike said. "Just thought you might have an idea I could work on."

"Not a one."

"I don't know how it's to be done, either. But I'll try."

"*Bueno!*" Brokus slapped him feebly. "*Bueno* to hell!"

He was dead in less than an hour. Mike took his gun and the better of the two horses, and rode down out of the hills, wishing he had some help. A lone hand didn't stand much whack, going against Roone's victorious mob up on the conquered Alta Mesa — if that was where Roone had taken Flame.

Not much whack at all. But there was nobody else left to try.

XIV
Two to Storm the Mesa

In the hope of borrowing some ammunition, Mike took an extra chance and dropped in at the Caven place. Being supposedly unarmed at the wedding, he and the Alta Mesa men had left off their gunbelts, carrying a few shells loose in their pockets.

Lindsay and Jana Caven stared at him as if seeing a ghost when he walked in on them as they were finishing supper. He had come up warily without their hearing him, a gun ready, not knowing what to expect.

"Anyone here besides you two?"

"No."

"Good." He began a brief account of what had happened, but they already knew.

"We had a visitor," Lindsay told him. "An Alta Mesa man, wounded and in a hurry. Gave us the story and begged a fresh horse. His was lamed by a bullet. What a shootout that must have been! He said you and

Brokus got cut off and left behind, or something; he wasn't sure because he and others rode into an ambush. Not many broke through, I gather, and they're skinning out of the country before Roone's Regulators go on the hunt for them tomorrow. How about Brokus himself?"

"Dead. Alta Mesa is finished, ready for Triangle T to loot."

Lindsay nodded. "A bunch of them passed a mile off, early in the evening, riding toward there. We haven't heard them come back. Where's Brokus' daughter?"

"She was with that same bunch, I expect. Roone would take her along, if only to show where Brokus kept his money."

"Mmm, yes, if only that." The Cavens looked carefully away from Mike's face. "Any guards up there?"

"Three, counting Ould Burro. No opposition, that, to the Roone crowd." Mike stuck his gun away. "It was quite a wedding," he said somberly.

"Glad you survived it, anyway. What do you need?"

"Gunbelt and shells. And I could use a drink."

Lindsay looked embarrassed. "Sorry. Not a drink left in the house. I'm — er — experimenting with sobriety. Coffee?

Jana . . ."

"I'll heat it up. Sit down, Mr. McLean."

"Thanks." Mike sank tiredly into a chair.

"The mail came in this morning at Fifty," Lindsay remarked. "There was a letter for us from Peter Hardy. You know, he left so quick, he didn't tell anyone where he raised the money to take Boy Pete to the hospital. He tells us in his letter. Mike, I bow to you!"

Mike glanced at the coffeepot. "I bet that's about hot now, Jana. How's Pete, did Hardy say?"

"The doctors say Pete will be all right," she replied, raising radiant eyes. "He won't be crippled."

He watched her pour the coffee. And, forgetting his manners, he ground out an oath. "Goddammit! If these folks only had some sense! And guts! Here's their chance! Roone's men will get drunk tonight celebrating, you can bet. These Middle Range cowmen could get the jump on 'em. After tonight it'll be too late. Roone will take their range and run 'em off. The damn fools!"

Lindsay regarded him strangely. "Why bother about them? If you showed your face in Fifty they'd try to tear you apart. Think of yourself, man! You've got some fast traveling to do tonight, like our wounded visitor!"

"Me? No." Mike drank the coffee. "I'm going up on Alta Mesa. It's why I want the shells."

Lindsay exchanged a solemn look with his sister. He slapped his hands on the supper table, sighed, and got up. "I was afraid of that. All right, I'll get them."

He returned carrying two broad gunbelts, double holstered, all shell loops filled. Mike said, "One's enough."

"The other one," Lindsay said gently, "is for me. I'm a good shot, remember. Two boneheads are better than one."

"Now look here! You're not doing any such —"

"Oh, shut up, you madman! I wouldn't do it if I weren't so stinking sober. And that's your doing if you want to know. I'll go saddle my horse." Lindsay hurried out of the house, buckling on his gunbelt.

Mike turned to Jana. "Can't you stop him?"

She was pale, but she shook her head. "Could anyone stop you?"

"It's different with me, Jana. I'm pledged."

"So is he, Mike. Pledged to prove himself. This is his chance to rise above his weaknesses and failures, don't you see?"

"Even if it kills him, as it most likely will?"

"Even so."

■ ■ ■ ■

They climbed up the path that Flame had shown to Mike on the night of the *baile*. Cautiously leaving their horses a mile back, they had approached the mesa on foot, trusting that Roone hadn't seen any reason to post lookouts on this high side.

The arroyos, bent by rock outcrops, forked into one another, the ascent steep and sliding in places. Lindsay Caven puffed like a spent runner. Reaching the top, Mike paused to get his bearings and crawled onto level ground. "You okay?" he whispered back.

"God, no!" gasped Lindsay. "Whiskey's poor training for toiling up a cliff in the dark, and this gunbelt weighs a ton! But I'm still with you, fool that I be. I perceive welcome lights ahead. The Brokus house?"

"Yeah. I don't speak for any welcome. Quiet now!"

Mike prowled wide around the house with slow care, examining all shadows before moving on. Close behind him, Lindsay murmured, "You were right about the drinking."

Loud voices of many men issued from the immense dining room. The lighted windows were unshuttered and open for air. There was the sound of a bottle smashed on the floor, a drunken whoop, and increased laughter. Roone was a strict boss, but tonight he was allowing his men free rein to celebrate the victory of Triangle T — Mike doubted if Roone could have kept them from drinking.

The clatter of a dishpan came from the open door of the kitchen, and curse delivered in an Irish brogue. Lindsay smothered a chuckle. Mike took a long look at all the lighted windows before he sprinted to the kitchen door. He halted there, listening, and peered in.

"Mr. O'Burrifergus," he said hushedly, "you're a hell of a servant! I saw you spit in that wine glass!"

Ould Burro rocked around, nearly tangling his feet. "Michael, I thought ye were dead! What in God's name d'ye do here? Yer life's not worth tuppence now! They've took over the whole —"

"Hold your voice down." Mike eased into the kitchen. "Have you gone over to them? Gone to work for them?"

"That's a low aspersion on me high character!" husked Ould Burro. "Some shootin' disturbed me slumber. When I woke up, they were grinnin' at me. They've made me their lackey, goddamn 'em! From their talk I fear ye all took a bad lickin' at Triangle T."

"The worst. A wipe-out. I'm all that's left, far as I know."

"I'll get ye a drink."

"Not in that glass. How's Flame? She's here, isn't she?"

"Aye, that she is. They brought her with 'em." In the dining room there was a crash and a renewed roar of laughter, and another crash. "They'll wreck the place. Roone's lettin' 'em do what they please. He's tryin' to show he's human, this night." Ould Burro filled the wine glass and set it on a tray. "Wine for his lordship!" he snorted. "Hah! Takes more'n a weak drink an' a stingy smile to make a man of a mackerel!"

Lindsay, slipping into the kitchen after Mike, commented, "A true observation."

Ould Burro bushed his brows at him. "You, is it? An' cold sober? Begod, now I know everything's topsy-turvy!"

"Is Flame in there?" Mike asked.

"She was. Roone ordered she must drink straight from a bottle. To belittle her, y'know. Make her act common like a slut. She flung the bottle at his face. Missed, unfortunately. Then she snatched a man's gun an' tried to shoot him, but it was no go."

Lindsay pursed his lips in a silent whistle. "Did he chastise the bride for her — hum — display of domestic dissatisfaction?"

"Chastise a wildcat? He had to have help to hustle her off to her room an' lock her in. She was a handful! I've heard some jokes whispered behind his back, about what further help he'll need. Grins an' nudges. They're a bad lot. I'm in horror for that gal. Roone only looks on her as —"

"Her room," Mike interrupted. "Upstairs, isn't it?"

"On the second floor." Ould Burro lifted the tray. "An' you know how this house is built. To go upstairs you got to pass through the dinin' room, there, no other way. What chance o' that?" He shrugged. The wine glass tipped precariously on the tray. "Git out o' here while ye're alive, the two of ye! Beat it! I got me damn job to do, servin' wine to his lordship, washin' glasses an' — arrgh!" He shouldered on through the inside door and bore the tray into the noisy dining room.

Lindsay, backing out of the kitchen, murmured to Mike, "Stay here." His eyes shone, intensely bright.

"What are you up to?"

"Going to try an idea. Just wait a bit."

Left alone, Mike listened to the din of the

174

revelers. They were throwing things around, hilariously destructive. It crossed Mike's mind that Lindsay had quit him, had pulled out of a hopelessly lost cause, with shamed regret. But presently four shots and a wild squawl disrupted the Triangle T revelry.

A second of stunned silence preceded the angry uproar of Roone's men piling out to get at the prowler who dared to shoot through a window at them.

"There he goes — there round the quarters!" A gun spat rapid reports. "Hell, he made it!"

"Must be crazy!"

"Would it be Brokus? He's a —"

"Naw, ol' Brokus got too damaged! McLean, more likely!"

"Go after him, you drunken fools!" snapped Roone's voice in chill wrath. "Get him, whoever he is!" As long as an enemy remained alive and active on Alta Mesa, Roone couldn't feel secure. Complete security was his goal. He had schemed ruthlessly to attain it, and now a madman pitted a threat to its final perfection. It was exasperating. "Find him and kill him!" he called after the running footsteps.

"Try an' find him in the dark!" one of the men was drunk enough to call back. "This place is full o' —"

"Search everywhere, damn your insolence!"

Mike opened the inside door and poked his head into the dining room. Its only occupant was Ould Burro, rising from a litter of overturned chairs and broken glass, the tray empty in his hand. He had got bowled over and stepped on in the rush.

"Lindsay fooled me that time!" he growled, flinging the tray down disgustedly. "He *is* drunk!"

"No," Mike said. "He did that to draw 'em out so I could get through here."

"Then he's as harebrained as you are! Get upstairs, quick! Her room's on the left, third door — may the saints help the pair o' ye!"

The staircase led up onto an inner gallery where the only source of light was the stairhead, from the lamplight in the big room below.

Mike tried the third door on the left. Due to the semi-darkness of the corridor, he couldn't tell at first what held it shut. There wasn't any lock, nor doorknob. The inside doors of Spanish-Southwest houses rarely had locks. Nor the outer doors, for that matter. This was a country of hand-wrought iron latches, and of wooden bars that the householder slotted into place at night if he happened to think of it.

176

Mike felt the iron latch. It was fastened with a twist of wire in lieu of a lock, so that the latch couldn't be raised from inside. By then his hurried fumblings caught the attention of Flame. Her tense whisper came muffled through the door.

"Who's that?"

"Me — Mike McLean."

"You? Oh, Mike — !"

"Quiet!"

Downstairs, a door banged. Footsteps clacked on the floor of the dining room. They paused. A gunshot blared. There was the sound of a body falling, then Ould Burro asking in pain-shocked tones, "Why did ye do that, Mr. Roone? Why did ye shoot me?"

"You know why!" came Roone's reply. "Somebody ran through here from the kitchen — I saw his shadow!"

"That was me! I —"

"Liar! It was a tall shadow crossing a window! Your friend McLean, wasn't it?"

"No, no! On me oath —"

"Yes, you old tramp, it was!" Roone raised his voice, calling out, "Come back here, men! Hurry! McLean's got into the house!"

Mike tore the twisted wire off the latch and threw open the door. Before him Flame's face was dim in the darkness, her figure framed by a pale oblong of window. The darkness didn't hide the shine of her eyes, and he thought she must be smiling, which didn't astonish him. Her nature and bizarre environment had combined to give her an extraordinary resiliency, an ability to adapt readily to changes of circumstances, and a sense of values stripped to essentials.

"You all right?"

"Yes, Mike. My father?"

"He died."

She said nothing for the space of a breath. Then, "Can you spare me a gun?"

"Here. What's outside your window?"

"A gallery and a long drop to the ground. Roone had the window nailed shut. I'd have broken it and tried a jump, but the noise . . ."

"Can't be helped. They'll search for me here first, anyway. Break it and climb out. I'll lower you down off the gallery. They're getting back!"

The returning men swarmed into the living room. One, incredulous like the rest, blurted, "You must be mistook, Mr. Roone! He couldn'ta got in the house! We chased —"

"He slipped around you! I think he's upstairs!" Roone rapped. "Get after him!"

A group of them came footing up the

staircase, as briskly purposeful as a military squad. By their unwary briskness they betrayed their disbelief in Roone's alarm. The lone prowler, chased off, couldn't have got into the house.

Mike tripped a cocked hammer. The flash and ringing report of the discharged shell abruptly shattered their disbelief. The foremost two topping the stair-head ducked automatically and jumped back, colliding into those pressing up behind them. The noise then resembled that of a disorganized squad tumbling downstairs. It almost smothered the noise made by Flame, bashing a chair at the bedroom window.

"Drunken oafs!" Roone tongue-lashed the cursing tangle of men. "I told you he was up there! You, Osbee — show me what you can do!"

"You bet, Mr. Roone!"

A man leaped up the stairs into the corridor, two guns blazing. Mike pulled his head in, rocked back on his knees, and prepared for the one-man army to come charging abreast of Flame's door. But another door along the corridor slammed open, and the two guns quit.

Flame spoke behind Mike. "That was Osbee — Roone's new ramrod. He's in the next room. We can't get out while he's there.

Its window opens onto the outside gallery, same as mine. He's waiting for us to try."

"Take my place here for a minute while I — What's that he's yelling?"

"He's telling some of them to run around to my little *placita,* below the gallery. It's the only spot where I've been able to raise a garden." Flame took Mike's place in the doorway. She swept her hair back, fired a shot at the stair-head, and said resignedly, "They'll trample my flowers."

Her mind wasn't on flowers, though, Mike knew. With trifles she was trying to stem a draining of optimism. He and she were trapped tight.

XV
POWDERSMOKE PROPHET

He went to the broken window and peered out at the gallery for a sight of Osbee. Instantly, Osbee's bullet splintered the window frame. Mike drew back and plucked a sliver from his cheek.

"Fast and ready," he muttered. "Did he shut that door behind him?"

"I didn't hear it shut," Flame said to him.

He bent over her. "Here are some extra shells. Keep your gun busy at the stairs! Keep 'em down shy!"

He stepped past her and moved swiftly along the corridor. A gun flared at him. The men on the stairs weren't shy, were only waiting for their ramrod's call to rush; and Mike, though crouched, made too tall a target to go unseen in the corridor above them.

The bullet got him high, tearing through the muscles between left shoulder and neck. It caused him to jerk aside. He skidded on the worn-over heels of his boots and slid along the wall. The door of the next room hung wide open. Off-balance, he fell through.

Osbee, at the room's window, spun around and fired immediately. His reactions were lightning fast, undulled by his drinking. He must have marked the doorway in his awareness as a prime danger spot.

What he hadn't taken into consideration was the implausible event of an intruder floundering into the room in a headlong sprawl. His bullets pocked the opposite wall of the corridor at the height of a man's chest. He then hesitated for a fraction of a second.

Mike got off a shot from the floor and heard Osbee hiss. He fired again, a foot higher. Osbee fell back to the open window, triggering a last shot that speared upward as he capsized across the windowsill. Mike checked a third shot, saving it. Osbee was finished.

He crawled out over the dead ramrod onto the gallery. Looking down, he saw the pattern of a small garden, adobe walls enclosing it on three sides, a picket fence with a gate through which men were trampling into the little *placita*. He darted along the gallery and climbed through the broken window into Flame's room. "There go your flowers!" he said to Flame.

She turned her face up to him. "You're hurt!"

"Some," he admitted. His left shoulder and arm dripped blood. She couldn't fail to see it. He knelt down beside her at the doorway. "I'll take this. You watch the window. They might try climbing up. D'you know any way to get out of here?"

"Only by digging through the wall and getting up to the top floor, then the roof. Give me your knife."

"Sorry; lost it in the blacksmith shed. Guess we stay here, Flame, long's we can."

"Guess we do, Mike," she said. A pause, and she added, "Thanks for coming to me. My father would have thanked you."

He spent a shell to flay the stair-head. "Him? No. Too tough. Gave me orders right to the last. I kind of liked him, though. We could've got along."

"He kind of liked you, too, Mike." She looked out the broken window at her little garden below being ruined by careless feet. " 'To guard the interests of me and mine,' " she quoted. "You stayed with it all the way. You kept your pledge."

"My pledge?" he grunted. He thumbed two shots savagely at a head that bobbed above the stairs. "Dammit, girl, don't talk that way to me! I don't need any pledge to send me searching for you tonight. Your father knew that. I told him so. Lindsay Caven didn't give any pledge, but he came with me. There are good men in the world, even here. Lindsay's one, whatever folks say about him. And by God, I'm another! Yes, me — Mike McLean!"

Born of hopelessness, a flaring passion torched the curtain of his reserve and self-control.

"Good enough to come after you, girl! To kill any man in my way! Good enough to take you for mine — yes, at any cost! Damn the pledge! I came here for you, understand?" he rasped at her.

"You're making it clear, Mike. Go on. Suppose things were different?" she asked.

Brazenly frank, he answered, "I'd take you off and keep you close to me. Your nights would never be lonely." Modesty didn't matter now. "I'd show you how to live to the full, and you'd show me, man and woman together."

His forthright reply brought tears to her eyes. " 'Come live with me, and be my love,' " she quoted softly. " 'And we shall all the pleasures —' "

Incredibly, in the big downstairs room

Ould Burro chanted like a carnival barker, "Gintlemen, step right here an' have yer fortunes told!"

The incongruous invitation caused a momentary hush, broken by some laughs from among the Triangle T men in the dining room and crowding the stairs.

"Come, come!" Ould Burro went on. " 'Tis yer chance in a lifetime! I've got the ancient Celtic gift o' prophecy that's granted to a dyin' Irishman. Nor do I ask ye to cross me palm wid silver — 'twould buy nothin' on me dark journey or at me final destination. Mr. Roone, where be ye? Me eyes ain't so good. Ah, there ye be, sir, I think, under the stairs."

"Shut your mouth!" said Roone.

"Surely a big man o' power like yerself don't fear to peek through the veil at yer future fortune?"

"My fortune's in my own hands, you old fraud!"

"Deed, aye," Ould Burro agreed, "an' a grand fortune it is. It could be mighty grander, who knows? 'There is a tide in the affairs o' men, which, taken at the flood, leads on to fame an' fortune,' as Bacon wrote."

"Shakespeare," Roone corrected him automatically.

"Was it, now? That feller wrote everything. I bow to yer superior education. Mine's rusty from long neglect. Let me foretell the future flood tide in yer affairs, so ye'll know when to take it. Ye're too wise, I'm sure, not to admit the possibility o' mystic divination. A closed mind is an ignorant mind."

Silence then, except for the purr of a riffled pack of cards. The Triangle T men were evidently watching, intrigued by Ould Burro's claim to clairvoyance and by his persuasive talk, curious to hear more.

Mike couldn't tell what the effect was on Roone. That coldblooded skeptic surely was immune to the cajoling patter of a fortune-telling cardsharp. Yet Roone wasn't voicing any further scornful objections. Perhaps Ould Burro, sly assessor of men's weaknesses, had detected in him a trace of superstition. Some of the most hard-headed men secretly paid a tithe of credence to palmistry, astrology, or just hunches. Even Napoleon had believed in his star of destiny.

"Three times shuffle, an' three times cut wid the left hand," intoned Ould Burro. "Now I deal five cards, placin' 'em in the form of a cross — the ancient Celtic manner which guards the significator from evil spirits. The significator bein' yerself, Mr. Roone. The imps o' Satan must be foiled

186

off, or they'd do their mischief in the divination."

"Cut the cackle an' get on with it!" somebody told him.

"The art of prognosis is not to be rushed, me good man," he returned severely. "Quiet! Here's the first card. A splendid card. Mr. Roone! It's the coverin' influence on yer fortune. The second card crowns it. Better an' better! The third goes beneath it. Hum! Let me concentrate."

He apparently concentrated.

"Ah, yes! A card denoting high ambition. How true! The next b'longs behind, an' it denotes strong effort in your recent past. The fifth shows what's before ye. Look, it's the ace o' diamonds! Most fortunate man! Now, sir, 'tis you must cut the deck yerself."

"Why?"

"An occult law. Ye make yer own fortune, as ye truly said. The card ye cut for yerself decrees the final result o' what these five show. It'll be a good card, I fancy, yer affairs bein' at flood tide, so have no fear. Come an' cut the deck. Are ye afraid, Mr. Roone? Afraid to face yer future? Afraid o' me, a dyin' ol' man wid one foot in the grave an' the other on a banana peel? For shame! Hold yer gun on me, then, if it'll

187

comfort ye."

The men muttered and shifted restlessly. Footsteps paced to the massive dining table. Roone couldn't take ridicule and loss of respect. "Give me the cards!"

"There ye are, sir. I thank ye for yer co-operation. . . ."

A muffled shot thudded, unmistakably discharged from a derringer, stubby muzzle pressed in direct contact with a body; a sleeve pistol in the conjuring hand of a man whose dimming eyesight required a point-blank target.

"An' there's yer future, ye black-souled mackerel — wid the compliments o' Timothy Sean Mario O'Burrifergus, Esquire!"

All sound and movement within the house stilled so completely that Mike had a weird feeling that he was suddenly struck deaf, that the ringing silence was unreal. He crept into the corridor to the head of the staircase and peered down.

The stillness was real. The men on the stairs and below in the dining room were staring frozenly at the huge table as if they couldn't believe their eyes. Their respect for Amery Roone personally wasn't overly high, but they had boundless respect for his power, his relentless force, his machine-like brain. He was the supreme head of a cattle empire, their proud outfit, invincible.

It wasn't credible that his guarded life should be snuffed out in the flick of an instant, by a broken-down old tinhorn gambler playing a last card trick. It couldn't be.

But the upper part of Roone's body lay limp on the table, face down, Ould Burro seated grinning dimly at it, the skimpy pistol smoking in his hand. Roone's outstretched forefinger rested on the sixth and final card of his fortune, the ace of spades. Ould Burro had stacked the deck. A matter of habit, finesse, and grim humor.

Rage flared. It swept through the staring Triangle T men simultaneously, a release from stunned disbelief. Cursing staccato, chopped-off oaths, they hammered shots at the shabby old figure. Ould Burro slid to the floor, dragging a scatter of cards with him. Their guns went on blaring senselessly at his riddled body, until of one accord the men in the room, tardily realizing the waste, craving another to spend vengeance on, charged the stairs, jostling those already there.

Some further gunfire and commotion sounded outside behind the house. Flame's little *placita,* Mike thought. No more flowers for this place. The Brokus stronghold

189

was ended: the Triangle T mob, leaderless, beserk, would demolish it, burn it down.

Firing, he retreated back along the corridor to Flame's room. A man lunged up from the stairs, snarling gutteral words. Mike's bullet toppled him rearward. The next one up threw a shot while slithering around on the floorboards and jumping down.

It was a fluke snapshot, guided by the instinctive accuracy of a hurried man in danger.

The bullet parted Mike's hair and rang bells in his head. He lurched sidewise and fell over, his gun scraping the floor. The firing behind the house increased, which dully puzzled him. He heard Flame, crouching beside him, saying with fervently desperate appeal, "Hold up, Mike! Don't die! I'll take care of you! I will — I will! Please don't die!"

"Watch the stairs!" he managed to say. "I'll be okay in a minute. Watch for 'em to —"

"They're leaving the stairs! Leaving the house!"

He didn't believe that. She must be mistaken. "Keep your head. Don't be scared." Empty encouragement. The enraged Triangle T men would ravage like wild animals.

"I w-won't be scared, Mike, if you'll get up!"

He got up clumsily, banging against her, against the doorframe, fumbling to cock the hammer of his gun, forgetful of what shells were left in the cylinders, if any.

"What're they shooting at outside? Why don't they come up?"

"I don't know."

They spoke against a rising roar of noise, gunshots studding the sounds of men vacating the house and then mingling in what sounded like a running fight with a lot of yelling.

"They're hog-wild," Mike said muddledly. "You and me, girl, are the only ones that've got any sense left. Everybody else is utter-to-bedamned crazy!"

"Mike, don't go to the stairs! Stay here!"

"Got to see what's going on, don't I?" It seemed clearly reasonable to him.

The stairs and dining room were empty of life, though not of death. He swayed on the landing, saying to Flame, she clinging to him, "I remember and regret I never even kissed you. Before they come back —"

"McLean! Where are you?" A man plunged through the gaping door into the big room, others behind him. They carried rifles and shotguns.

"I'm right here," Mike answered distinctly.

The shouting man resembled Ed Horner, but that could only be a trick of imagination. Although Mike's eyes didn't focus straight, his head felt perfectly clear.

"Shoot, you yappers!" he said. A clean death for Flame and for himself. Clicking his emptied gun, he tumbled down the stairs, Flame still clinging onto him. His perfectly clear head went spinning into blackness.

"After I stirred up the Roone jamboree here," Lindsay Caven said, "I skedaddled off the mesa as fast as I could in the dark. I'm no flaming hero," he admitted.

"You'll do," Mike commented sparely. He sat on the bottom stair, groggily, while Flame cut away the remains of his shirt and tried to decide where to begin patching him up.

"Thanks," Lindsay acknowledged. "As a last resort I headed for Fifty, to stir *them* up next, if I could. But I met them coming here. I don't know yet what brought them. Haven't had time to ask, too busy showing them the way up — and then one thing and another when we got here."

"Your sister, it was," stated Ed Horner. "Godamighty! She rode into Fifty an' told us off. Showed us a letter from Peter Hardy. The letter was an eye-opener, but the names Miss Jana called us — who-ee! I disremember some. You, Mr. Sord?"

Thomas Sord, an unobtrusive man with earnest eyes, who was reputed to be a disbarred lawyer from Boston, cleared his throat with a dry cough. " 'Weak trash,' " he related specifically. " 'No more backbone than, er, dough-splatter. Worthless. Not men at all. Tick-fevered dogies. Psalm-singing hypocrites.' The rest of it I didn't hear, because of my wife, who told me — er, advised me, I mean — that strong action was required. Miss Jana also said that now was the time to strike for our, er, homes and liberty. A forceful phrase!"

"You'll like Jana," Mike assured Flame, "when you get to really know her. Jana's okay."

"I'm sure of that," she responded with only the slightest edge of feminine rivalry, wanting his whole regard. "I want to belong with these Middle Range folks — to belong to you! Am I shameless, Mike?"

"You're shameless, all right," he said in her ear, "and you're going to belong to me — our wedding night, or whatever. I'll be as shameless as you! I'll make love to you like no girl has ever been made love to before!"

"Hold still!" she whispered, coloring hotly, dabbing at his shoulder wound. Her eyes were velvet stars.

"Those Regulators!" Ed Horner jeered. "Gunmen! We sure did ki-yi 'em off! Shoulda done it long ago. O' course McLean," he conceded, "you'd already took care o' Roone."

"Not me," said Mike. He got up and weaved a course to the center table, Flame at his side. He gazed down at a rascally, dead old face.

"Hats off to Mr. Timothy O'Burrifergus! Hats off, I say, all of you! Pay respects to him, a good man!"

The hats came off. Mike steadied himself, leaning partly on Flame, partly on the table. Anger came over him, anger at the stolid prejudice of self-righteous men.

"You all looked down your goddamn noses at him!" he accused them harshly. "A boozy old tinhorn, eh? Well, that was my friend. You belittled my girl, called her the Cheyenne Flame. You cussed me for a dodger on the make. All right! But if it wasn't for us —"

Flame tugged at his arm. "Mr. McLean isn't quite himself, as you can see," she broke in quickly to save him from saying bitter things that would burn and rankle.

194

The Middle Range cowmen had come through in the final pinch, and recriminations for past failings could only do harm. "He's hurt."

"I sure am! As I was saying —"

"What he means is, let's not have any more bad feeling. Let's be neighbors and friends. Forget the grudges. Let's just trust each other and get along."

He looked at her. "Did I mean that?"

"Of course you did!" She wiped his face possessively, tenderly careful of her man. "The whole range is open now for all of us to use. The trails out to market are wide open. If," she said, "you agree, Mike."

"Me? Honey, you're queen of the Triangle T and Alta Mesa, and —"

"You're king! It's your word that counts, don't you see? I'm yours, all yours, every particle of me! I'll always be yours, your woman, wife, mistress — I don't care! I'm a female, glad to find my man."

From then on there arose considerable talk and much crowding around on the part of the Middle Range cowmen. In victory they were boisterous, taking most of the credit for themselves.

However, some of them did say respectfully, "Miss Brokus," when addressing her. A few others said, "Miss Flame."

It didn't seem to occur to anyone to call her Mrs. Roone, a recently bereaved widow. Amery Roone lay dead; his hired toughs were scamping off to other parts, their paydays cut off, no further loyalty to the outfit entailed. Mike went and picked up Ould Burro's battered hat.

"I'll keep this. He brushed broken glass from its dented crown and placed it on the table. "It'll always remind me of — of . . ." At a loss for words, he lowered his eyes to the roguish old face grinning serenely on the floor.

"He was a gentleman," said Lindsay Caven, coming to his aid. "An Irish gentleman of the old stock."

" 'Deed, aye, as he'd have said," Mike added as he put his arm around Flame.

"Mike!" she breathed into his ear, cuddling readily into his arm. "Let's — let's . . ." She blushed crimson, her longing for him so naked.

"Let's get somewhere out of this crowd," Mike said to her, and she preceded him upstairs, her figure erect and proud. "Lord, hide your blushes!"

At daybreak, the house empty, he said to her, "Will you marry me, Flame? Today?"

"Why, of course," she murmured drowsily. "Anything you want, Mike." She turned to him, pressing her lithe young body to his.

"I'll marry you, gladly. Besides, I'd better, after last night!"

" 'Live with me and be my love . . .' "

"Yes, Mike! Oh, yes, yes!"

ABOUT THE AUTHOR

L(eonard) L(ondon) Foreman was born in London, England in 1901. He served in the British army during the Great War, prior to his emigration to the United States. He became an itinerant, holding a series of odd jobs in the western States as he traveled. He began his writing career by introducing his most widely known and best-loved character, Preacher Devlin, in "Noose Fodder" in *Western Aces* (12/34), a pulp magazine. Throughout the mid thirties, this character, a combination gunfighter, gambler, and philosopher, appeared regularly in *Western Aces*. Near the end of the decade, Foreman's Western stories began appearing in Street & Smith's *Western Story Magazine,* where the pay was better. Foreman's first Western novels began appearing in the 1940s, largely historical Westerns such as *Don Desperado* (1941) and *The Renegade* (1942). The *New York Herald Tribune* reviewer commented on *Don Desperado* that "admirers of the late beloved Dane Coolidge better take a look at this. It has that same all-wool-and-a-yard-wide quality." Foreman continued to write prolifically for the magazine market as long as it lasted, before specializing exclusively for the book trade with one of his finest novels, *Arrow in the Dust* (1954) which was filmed under this title the same year. Two years earlier *The Renegade* was filmed as *The Savage* (Paramount, 1952), the two are among several films based on his work. Foreman's last years were spent living in the state of Oregon. Perhaps his most popular character after Preacher Devlin was Rogue Bishop, appearing in a series of novels published by Doubleday in the 1960s. George Walsh, writing in *Twentieth Century Western Writers,* said of Foreman: "His novels have a sense of authority because he does not deal in simple characters or simple answers." In fact, most of his fiction is not centered on a confrontation between good and evil, but rather on his characters and the changes they undergo. His female characters, above all, are memorably drawn and central to his stories.

We hope you have enjoyed this Large Print book. Other Thorndike, Wheeler, Kennebec, and Chivers Press Large Print books are available at your library or directly from the publishers.

For information about current and upcoming titles, please call or write, without obligation, to:

Publisher
Thorndike Press
295 Kennedy Memorial Drive
Waterville, ME 04901
Tel. (800) 223-1244

or visit our Web site at:

http://gale.cengage.com/thorndike

OR

Chivers Large Print
published by BBC Audiobooks Ltd
St James House, The Square
Lower Bristol Road
Bath BA2 3SB
England
Tel. +44(0) 800 136919
email: bbcaudiobooks@bbc.co.uk
www.bbcaudiobooks.co.uk

All our Large Print titles are designed for easy reading, and all our books are made to last.